Crypto

A JOHN WESLEY O'TOOLE NOVEL

ALSO BY WILLIAM RAWLINGS

PUBLISHED BY MERCER UNIVERSITY PRESS

The Columbus Stocking Strangler (2022)

Lighthouses of the Georgia Coast (2021)

Six Inches Deeper (2020)

The Girl with Kaleidoscope Eyes (2019)
(A John Wesley O'Toole Novel)

The Strange Journey of the Confederate Constitution (2017)

The Second Coming of the Invisible Empire (2016)

A Killing on Ring Jaw Bluff (2013)

PREVIOUSLY PUBLISHED

The Mile High Club (2009)

Crossword (2006)

The Tate Revenge (2005)

The Rutherford Cipher (2004)

The Lazard Legacy (2003)

Crypto

A JOHN WESLEY O'TOOLE NOVEL

William Rawlings

MERCER UNIVERSITY PRESS
Macon, Georgia

MUP/ P677

© 2023 by Mercer University Press
Published by Mercer University Press
1501 Mercer University Drive
Macon, Georgia 31207
All rights reserved

9 8 7 6 5 4 3 2 1

Books published by Mercer University Press are printed on acid-free
paper that meets the requirements of the American National
Standard for Information Sciences—Permanence of Paper for Printed
Library Materials.

Printed and bound in the United States.

Cover Design by Burty&Burt

This book is set in Adobe Garamond Pro.

ISBN   978-0-88146-903-5 (print)
ISBN   978-0-88146-904-2 (eBook)

Cataloging-in-Publication Data is available from the Library of
Congress

Crypto: From the Ancient Greek word κρυπτός (*kruptós*), meaning secret or hidden. Often used as a prefix to describe situations, organizations, individuals, or concepts whose purpose, motivation, and goals are unknown.

MERCER
UNIVERSITY PRESS

Endowed by
TOM WATSON BROWN
and
THE WATSON-BROWN FOUNDATION, INC.

AUTHOR'S PREFACE

John Wesley O'Toole, the disbarred attorney turned art dealer, returns again in *Crypto,* a work of suspense fiction set in the beautiful city of Savannah. Having recovered from the trauma of being arrested and charged with murder in the Abraham Deign episode as recounted in *The Girl with Kaleidoscope Eyes,* O'Toole is approached by Donald Moule, a pleasant, if peculiar, investment trader specializing in cryptocurrencies. O'Toole is uncertain about taking him on as a client until Moule reveals he wants to diversify his holdings by investing millions in high-quality works of art. As often seems to happen with opportunities that may appear too good to be true, matters become far more complicated than could ever be imagined, once again plunging O'Toole into mortal danger.

This work, like all in this series, is written as a stand-alone novel. Although I am confident readers will enjoy the previous work, having read it is not necessary to appreciate this tale of suspense. John O'Toole is a fascinating if imperfect character, and episodes from his unpredictable life will continue to appear in subsequent novels.

William Rawlings
Sandersville, Georgia
January 1, 2023

CHAPTER 1

I can't recall exactly when I first met Donald Moule. It was during those heady months that followed the end of the Deign affair when my upside-down world slowly began to return to some sense of normalcy. I do remember distinctly, however, being in my office at the gallery when Jessica, my one full-time employee, barged in to hand me a gilt-edged business card bearing the name of Donald D'Entremont-Moule, the single word "Consultant," and a telephone number. She looked a bit annoyed, glancing back to make sure the door was shut before speaking. "This guy says he wants to meet you"—then in a low voice—"Kinda weird-looking."

I turned the card over and examined it. Good linen paper stock, quality engraving. On the other hand there is an ill-defined flaw in my personality that triggers an innate distrust of anyone who describes himself as a "consultant" and has both an apostrophe and a hyphen in his last name. My first reaction was to tell Jessica to say I was tied up on a conference call, but before I could speak she continued, "He's been here several times—you were out. And he bought the Meadows pieces last month." My attitude immediately changed. It was a $5,500 sale of two paintings that had hung unsold in the gallery for more than a year.

"In that case, then…," I said and headed for the door with Jessica close behind me. Surveying the gallery, my first thought was that the man must have left. Then, just beyond a rack of art books, I saw a shiny dome bobbing up and down. I glanced toward Jessica. "He's kinda short and bald," she mouthed silently. I headed in his direction, rounding the book rack to see

1

a small, somewhat chubby bald man studying a coffee-table sized volume of Kabuki art. He looked up and smiled.

"Mr. O'Toole," he said warmly, sticking out his hand. "I'm Don Moule, and I'm really glad to meet you. I've heard a lot of good things about you and your gallery."

"Thank you," I replied. "It's good to meet you as well. Jessica told me you bought the Cora Dell Meadows paintings last month."

"Yes, a real bargain, I thought. California School, 1920s. Wonderful pieces for my collection. Thank you."

"I was fortunate to purchase them from an estate here in Savannah," I said, trying to get a feel for this odd little man. I glanced at his business card, still in my hand. "I don't want to mispronounce your name, is it 'D'Entremont-Moule' or 'Moule' or…"

"I'm sorry," he said, blushing a bit. "It's Moule. My family's originally from Canada, Nova Scotia to be exact. I go by Moule now. It's easier to pronounce—like 'mole.'"

"Oh, okay," I said, confused. "May I offer you a cup of coffee?"

We sat in my private office, Moule on the leather couch with his feet barely touching the carpet, me in my chair facing him. Moule was dressed in pleated wool slacks and a starched pinstripe shirt with the top two buttons undone, revealing the occasional glint of a gold chain hanging around his neck. A pair of glasses with thick black frames perched on his nose. He looked to be in his mid to late forties, perhaps a decade older than me. Jessica brought coffee as we made small talk. "So, you're a collector?" I asked.

"Yes, art is one of my passions," Moule said, smiling. "It's always been my dream to surround myself with works whose beauty transcends time. In the last few years that's finally become possible. I moved to Savannah from Albuquerque a couple of years ago—I think this will be my permanent home."

"I hope you don't mind my asking, but your card only says 'Consultant.' What sort of business are you in?"

Moule blushed again, his face and shiny scalp turning a deeper shade of pink. "Uh…computers basically. My degree— I have a PhD from Stanford—is in number theory and computational data management. It's a field that's in high demand in the business world."

"Oh," I replied, having no way to interpret what he had just said. I couldn't decide if he had deliberately given me a vague answer or if I was expected to ask further questions. He was a strange fellow to be sure. My prime concern was cultivating Moule as a client, so I elected to change the subject. If he wanted me to know more, I assumed he would tell me. "You mentioned your art collection. Is there one particular focus, one period, one genre or the like? I'd welcome the opportunity of helping you find good pieces."

"That would be great," Moule said, leaning forward on the couch. "In fact, that's why I wanted to meet you. Look, I'm planning to be in Savannah a very long time. It'd be good to have someone to help me—a consultant, really. The same thing I do for other people. They tell me what they want to do financially, and I help them reach their goals. I tell you where I want to go with my art, and you help show me the way. As I like to say to my clients, it's a win-win situation for both of us."

I nodded, still a bit uncertain despite what appeared to be an ideal business opportunity. Something in the back of my mind warned me to be careful.

CHAPTER 2

My conversation with Don Moule lasted about twenty minutes, yielding little additional information. We exchanged pleasantries and superficial comments on the difficulty of understanding the world of art. Moule seemed socially awkward and almost uncomfortable in a one-on-one conversation. His interest in art was something from his childhood, he said, vaguely referring to his mother's influence. He spoke of growing up playing video games, which in turn sparked a fascination with computers and eventually led to his doctorate, funded mainly by scholarships and jobs as a teaching assistant. I was pleasant, smiling and nodding, but rather than asking questions I waited for him to volunteer information. Eventually our discussion turned back to ways I could assist him with his collection. Moule started by trying to explain his interests but seemed frustrated in finding the right words, eventually saying, "Why don't you just come over to my place and let me show you what I've got. I think it'd be easier that way." We agreed to meet the next afternoon before parting with smiles and a handshake.

Jessica, who had been hovering unseen outside my office door, said, "So you're going to work with him?"

"Can't hurt," I replied. "We're in the business and he's a customer."

"He kinda gives me the creeps," she replied, unconsciously hugging herself. "I don't know what it is, but..." Her voice trailed off.

"We'll see," I said. "I'm meeting him tomorrow at his house."

"Umm," she replied and headed back to her desk.

I suppose you could describe Moule as creepy, but in truth, I needed the business. I had inherited the gallery and the big house on Liberty Street from my grandmother, the sole legacies of my life before prison. Sales were brisk at the moment, thanks in large part to the publicity generated through press coverage of the disappearance of Abraham Deign and his attempts to implicate me in his murder plot. One friend told me I had become a "sympathetic figure." At this point I didn't care. I had lost everything from the years before and was trying to rebuild my life. The art business is fickle, with highs and lows and long dry spells during economic downturns. If sympathy led to sales, so much the better. And if men like Don Moule wanted to purchase a painting or two, I would be glad to oblige.

Moule had given me an address on East Gaston Street in the downtown historic district. The area was only about a dozen blocks from the gallery and, for the most part, an upscale neighborhood of restored nineteenth century townhouses. The following afternoon was a perfect spring day, sunny with temperatures in the mid-seventies. I was in a good mood at the prospect of a new and hopefully well-paying buyer, and decided to enjoy the day by walking. Gaston Street marks the upper end of Forsyth Park, a vast greenspace in the heart of the city's historic district, its trees and manicured lawns punctuated by fountains and surrounded by the elegant homes of Savannah's wealthy from years past. Moule's home, a red-brick, three-story Victorian, appeared to have been recently restored with gleaming white marble trim and a newly installed slate roof. I pressed the bell button next to one of the massive oak double doors at the top of a set of brick steps. Moule appeared shortly, ushering me in with a smile. I was unprepared for what I saw next.

I was expecting to find the usual interior of such a house: wood paneling, thick mantels hand-carved from locally grown live oak, polished brass light fixtures, and wooden interior shutters to hide it all from the streetside eyes of the curious. But the local architectural review committees that hold sway over a home's exterior have no control over what an owner can do behind his thick historical walls. Instead of the usual heavy wood pocket doors separating the foyer from the formal living and dining rooms, it appeared that the interior of the first floor had been basically gutted, swept clean of all but the most essential weight-bearing walls, and then rebuilt as a single, bright, cavernous space. The one major exception was the massive staircase with its ornately carved newel post and balustrade ascending to the home's second level. The original wood floors had been preserved and extended to cover gaps where walls once stood. The exterior walls themselves, now painted pure white on the inside, were pierced by windows covered with thick curtains. The room glowed with a soft light emanating from a high shallow recess and reflecting off the white ceiling some fifteen feet above. Three fireplaces, each at one time serving to heat an individual room in the original house plan, now lined up along the outside wall. Each was adorned by a dark grey granite hearth and surround below a simple matching granite slab that served as a mantel. Several individual furniture groups were distributed around the space: two seating areas, one facing a massive wall-mounted video screen, another in front of the middle fireplace, and a third space consisting of a sleek dining room table and chairs near the rear. A nearby door presumably led to a kitchen.

The most striking aspect of the room was what hung on the walls. Each expanse of open space was adorned by a large colorful painting illuminated by a bank of pure white spotlights focused on it from the ceiling high above. I didn't immediately recognize the works as those of one particular artist or another. One large canvas covered with squiggly oils dashed in a faint flowing pattern resembled the work of Jackson Pollock. Another oversized cartoon figure of a weeping blonde was vaguely similar to a work of Roy Lichtenstein that I had once seen at an exhibition at the Museum of Modern Art in New York. In total, there were more than a dozen such canvases, each a colorful counterpoint to the neutral hues that otherwise defined the space, but otherwise lacking in a central theme or style.

Moule stood quietly, his arms crossed, as I observed the room in awe. "Amazing," I said, being truthful at least in part.

"They're not originals, you know, I mean by famous artists," Moule replied, grinning nervously. "Well, most of them aren't anyway. I have a few more valuable pieces upstairs." He paused, "These are as they say—'In the style of....' I couldn't begin to afford the real things when I was starting out, but business has been good lately. I want to do some serious investing, and I want you to help me."

Moule needed help. If I had finished my thought, I would have added, "This has to rate as one of the most gaudy, over-the-top displays I think I've ever seen." But I held my tongue. Moule continued, "I hired an architectural design firm out of Los Angeles to help me redo this house. They did some work for a client of mine in Albuquerque. Got great reviews in the local press. They did a terrific job here, huh?"

"It's certainly a great West Coast design," I observed, thinking the entire room would be a better fit for a Malibu beach house. Moule grinned. "Did the designers help choose the artwork as well?"

"Some of it, yeah. I've been buying pieces here and there. I had them stored in a climate-controlled locker before moving them here." He paused, surveying the room. "You know, you're really the first person from Savannah to see the finished product. I wanted to show it off to someone who I knew would appreciate it."

"Thank you. I'm honored," I lied, spending the next few minutes pretending to admire the paintings. "You said there were more?" I asked.

"Yes. Upstairs where I work. My office and bedroom are on the second floor, and I have a couple of guest rooms on the top level. Let's take the elevator," he said, pointing to a door at the rear of the stairs.

The next level was more conventionally designed. What had apparently been a bedroom at the front of the house was now a workspace illuminated primarily by the glow of banks of computer monitors from several separate workstations. A cluster of monitors displaying what appeared to be financial market data was mounted on one wall. "This is where I spend most of my days, and sometimes my nights, dealing with clients, doing research, that kind of thing."

"I see you've got more than one desk. Do you have an assistant or other employees?" I asked.

"Oh, no, just me. I sit here when I'm emailing or on a video call with clients," Moule said, pointing to one desk with its bank of monitors. "Over there is where I do most of my research," he said, pointing to another, "and this place here is where I do trading—buying and selling, that kind of thing, for myself and for clients." He pointed at the wall-mounted monitors. "From here I can watch the markets. You know how it is…"

I did not, and wasn't sure I wanted to.

"I've got my best pieces in my bedroom," Moule said, directing me toward the rear of the house. Here, too, it appeared that several smaller rooms had been gutted and then rebuilt into one large bedroom suite. A king-sized bed dominated the space. The floor was covered by a palace-sized Isfahan carpet while the walls, again white, were hung with a series of smaller, but no less colorful, canvases. We stood in the doorway. Moule said, "What do you think?"

"Really nice," I said.

"No, I mean about the art?"

I looked about the room. Most of the canvases appeared to be works copying abstract expressionists. Here was one that resembled a de Kooning; there was another that looked vaguely Pollock-ish. The most striking of all was a medium-sized rectangular canvas hung on the otherwise bare wall over the headboard of the bed. On a background of deep blue, the artist had painted two slightly irregular smaller rectangles, one orange, the other red. "Like I told you, I keep my best pieces here," Moule said. "The two Meadows paintings I bought from you are hung in the dressing room." He paused. "You recognize any of the artists?"

I wondered if he was testing me, but I was willing to play along. "Well, I'm not exactly certain, but that one there appears to be in the style of Pollock. And that one—"

"What about the one over the bed?" Moule interrupted.

I studied it for a moment. "I can't see a signature from across the room, but offhand I'd say it could be a Rothko."

Moule smiled. "You're good, John. Really good. You got it." He surveyed the room. "Oh, and I was told Rothko never signed his work."

I turned and looked at Moule, assuming the painting was a copy.

"So the artist wanted to copy more than just his style?"

Moule frowned. "No, I think you misunderstood me.

That's a work by Mark Rothko, painted in the early 1960s, before either one of us was born."

I couldn't read Moule's face. "You're serious?"

"Absolutely. I bought it at an estate sale in Santa Fe. They didn't know what they had, and I didn't bother to tell them. I had the folks at the National Gallery in Washington authenticate it."

"You realize, of course, what that would sell for…," I began.

"Seven figures, I'd guess, maybe more," Moule said, looking up at me with a sly smile. For an instant the spotlight glinting off his bald pate seemed to resemble a halo.

CHAPTER 3

An awkward moment of silence followed as Moule stared about the room at his collection. "None of this is real, you know," he said, looking a bit pensive.

"How do you mean?" I asked.

"Art. It's...well...it's just not real." He saw the puzzled look on my face. "It's like what I do every day, trading things online, buying and selling, following the markets. None of it's real." He gestured toward the paintings, his voice a shade louder. "Look at them, John. What do you see? Squares of canvas covered with paint smeared in various colors and patterns? Some of this stuff is so bad that a five-year-old kid with a paint set could have done it and you wouldn't know the difference. But here it is, in this strange world where things have value because we've all gotten together and agreed that they do." Moule was flushed now, gesturing with his arms as he spoke. "And sometimes you have to wonder if this all isn't just a terrible joke. That one day someone will knock on your door and say, 'Hey! This game's over—time to move on to the next one.'" Moule looked at me, waiting for my response.

I wasn't sure what to say. On a certain level he was correct, but I didn't want to offend him by saying that the concept could be applied to many things in life besides the value of art. My two years in prison had given me a long time to think about what is—and what's not—important. "You're right," I said, "but value translates to money, and money can buy other things."

"Yeah, but it's not just art, it's almost everything. It's about control. You mentioned money. Money has value because the government prints up little green pieces of paper and tells you it's worth something. And once you've bought into that, they track it through banks and stock exchanges and the like, and take it back in taxes and fees, and try to tell you both what you can and cannot do with it. They want to regulate your life." Moule was becoming agitated. He took a deep breath.

I didn't reply, waiting for him to continue.

"I'm sorry," Moule said, a bead of sweat appearing on his forehead. "I guess you see I have a hot button. It's the one thing I'm truly passionate about—helping people avoid the prying eyes of Big Brother. That's why I do what I do."

Once again, I had no idea what he was talking about and what any of this had to do with art. If what he was alleging about the paintings was true, he had at least one million-dollar-plus canvas hanging on the wall of his bedroom and was at the same time ranting about none of this being "real" and about the "prying eyes of Big Brother," whatever all that meant. For a fleeting moment the thought crossed my mind that he might be a true nutcase, or at the very least delusional and paranoid. It hit me that maybe I should try to extract myself from the situation at the earliest opportunity. I changed the subject. "You said you do online trading. I'd like to hear more. Is that at the heart of your consulting business?"

Now clearly embarrassed by his outburst, Moule said, "Yes…, er…let's talk about that." I followed him back to his workspace with its banks of monitors. He motioned to a leather couch and told me to make myself comfortable. He settled into a chair facing me and asked, "I presume you've heard of cryptocurrencies? Things like Bitcoin and Ethereum and Dogecoin and others?" I nodded. "How much do you know about them? Do you own any? Each one's a bit different, but do you understand in general how they work?" I said I did not.

"Then let me explain," he began.

For most of the next half hour I sat quietly while the short, bald, bespectacled Moule became the professor, trying to convince me that the US dollar—and most other world currencies for that matter—are worth something simply because we agree that they are. In the past, he pointed out, nations kept gold and silver reserves that theoretically backed up this value, but for most of the last century this has not been the case. This whole scheme, he said, is run through national banks. In the United States, the Federal Reserve System is in charge of the dollar; in Europe, the euro is controlled by the European Central Bank, and so on around the world. These central banks manipulate and control interest rates, money supply, and the like to keep the so-called value of their currency stable, but it comes with a catch. "Today, essentially every major transaction is—or can be—monitored by governmental agencies. Every time you use a credit card to buy gas, or pay with a check that is deposited in the banking system, or buy stocks or bonds—all this information is available to the so-called regulators, and to the bad guys who hack into their computer systems." He paused, as if waiting for that to sink in. Then, "There are some people out there, a lot of them in fact, who don't like it. That's why cryptocurrencies were born."

At this point, Moule lost me. I tried to appear interested and engaged as he began to discuss the concept of independent, self-regulating digital currencies managed on peer-to-peer networks, alternatives to the dollar, the euro, the yuan, and others but shielded from the prying eyes of governments and "insulated against hackers and other bad actors," as he called them. As his soliloquy started filling up with terms like fiat currency, blockchain, genesis block, cryptowallets, stablecoin, and

13

references to the writing of Satoshi Nakamoto—whom he casually mentioned was not a real person—I finally had enough.

"Don, listen," I interrupted him. "I really appreciate your trying to explain all this to me, but let me just say I think I understand the concepts and will leave the fine points to guys like you with PhDs. You said you were interested in my helping you find works for your collection. Am I correct in thinking that you want investment-quality art, something that will hold its value with time?"

Moule nodded, softly mumbling "Yes," on the realization that he had lost me somewhere in his attempts to explain the world's digital currencies in thirty minutes or less.

"Good. That's a beginning," I said. "Okay, two other questions and we can get started." Moule seemed to brighten a bit. "First, based on what I've seen, it looks like most of the works you have now fall in the broad category of abstract expressionism. Do you want me to look for things in that genre, or more generally? Of course, if I find something that I think may work, the first thing I'll do is send you a photo and info on the artist for your consideration."

"That will be good for a start. I'm mainly interested in works that will hold their value over time. This is going to be my retirement account," Moule said.

"Okay, we can do that. One more question: About how much do you want to invest to start, say in the next six months or so?"

"I'm not really sure," Moule replied, pursing his lips while he appeared to be considering things. "I spent a lot on this house, of course. I figured it would be a good investment, and I've got a few other things out there." Picking up a scrap of paper from the table beside his chair, he scribbled a few numbers and appeared to be doing some calculations. Looking back up, he said, "Let's go with a round number, say one million dollars in the first six months. After that, we can see how things go."

CHAPTER 4

One thing you need to know about the art business is that it's not a great way to become wealthy. To be sure, we've all heard the story of some suburban housewife finding an original Michelangelo at a yard sale and then selling it through Christie's for enough to retire and live comfortably for the rest of her life. It happens. If Moule was telling the truth, he had lucked into that sort of good fortune with his purchase of the alleged Rothko. But such apocryphal events are as rare as unicorns, and often just as real. To be clear, even though I love art in the abstract sense, I was not running an art gallery out of some dreamy attraction to its beauty or emotional impact. I was doing it because I inherited the gallery from my grandmother, and it was all I had after getting out of prison. I had been—in what seemed like another lifetime—a successful attorney, but that ended with my incarceration for felony vehicular homicide, the implosion of my marriage, and the loss of my law license that followed. Now, going on three years after my release, I was still in survival mode but determined to make a go of things, to earn success in another field.

Like the story of Moule's Rothko, his plan to spend a million dollars on investment-grade art sounded simply too good to be true. The fact that he had spent $5,500 on a couple of quality canvases initially excited me. The offer to spend nearly two hundred times that amount in the next six months both baffled and frightened me. Since I had taken over management of the gallery, my very best month brought in just below $50,000 in gross sales, with most bringing in far less. Factoring in my overhead that ran close to forty-five percent, the business was profitable but not in a major way. I was still paying on debts from my marriage and divorce, plus a generous amount for the support of two children I had not seen in years. I needed good, objective advice.

There were three people I knew I could count on. First, Jessica, who had worked at the gallery for more than a decade and who understood sales and knew our customers. Then there was Hattie, the gallery's longtime bookkeeper and general financial advisor. She would be the voice of experience and wisdom. And finally, I had Jenna, my friend, confidant, and sometimes lover. None of the three would be reluctant to give me their honest opinion, nor would they be in the least way hesitant to disagree with whatever course I was considering if they thought I was making a mistake.

I spoke with Jessica first. She sat quietly as I recounted my visit with Moule, nodding as she listened and occasionally asking for clarification. I went into some detail about his "collection" and told her as well as I could about his attempts to explain cryptocurrencies. When I said Moule wanted to invest a million dollars in high-grade art, Jessica gave a short, spontaneous gasp. After nearly fifteen minutes of nonstop talking I paused and asked, "What do you think?"

"John, I think I understand what he was trying to say. He must have made some big bucks somewhere—either through his consulting or his dealing with these cryptocurrencies, which I don't begin to understand. But no matter what he says, or how much money he offers you, I still think he's weird. I can't pick out one thing he's said or done, but just looking at the whole thing—it's not right. Either he's crazy or it's some sort of a scam."

"A bit crazy, perhaps, but what if we could verify, say, that he has the cash, or that the painting is really a Rothko?" I replied.

"Okay, that might give you some assurance, but it reminds me of those scam emails you get from Nigerian princes wanting you to…" Her voice trailed off when she saw my look.

"I really appreciate your thoughts," I said. "I want to see what Hattie thinks."

Hattie met me that evening at the gallery. We sat in my office, she with a cup of tea and me with coffee while I went over the events of the last few days. She listened quietly, her hair done tightly in her signature bun, her eyes focused sharply on me as I spoke. When I paused Hattie said, "I recognized Moule's name. I saw that he bought the Meadows paintings and thought you did well on that one. What brought him back to the gallery? I don't mean to say we're small potatoes, but if he's serious and really has that kind of money to invest, it seems like he would head for New York or London or Paris. I know we both love Savannah, but relatively speaking this is a small town and a long way from the centers of the art world. Why did Moule move here in the first place?"

"I have no idea," I replied. "And I don't know why, out of all the galleries in the city, he chose to come to mine."

"Hmm," Hattie said, her lips pursed. "I'm familiar with cryptocurrencies. You know we're required to do continuing education to keep our accounting licenses, and that's been a big topic in our review courses for a few years now. He could have easily made a lot of money—I believe you said he has a PhD in number theory and data management. All these new digital currencies would be right up his alley, but"—she hesitated before she continued as if to choose her words carefully—"there are a lot of shady things going on out there. The crypto market is totally unregulated. From an investment perspective, it's like hanging out on the wrong side of the street on the wrong side of the tracks on the wrong side of town. The bad guys like it because they can move large sums of money around relatively undetected. And the hackers love it because when corrupt money is stolen, the folks that were the victims can't report it without incriminating themselves. Do you suppose Moule is trying to convert dirty money to other forms of investments that can be sold for legitimate cash? That's a textbook example of money laundering. You've got to realize that if something like that is going on and it all blows up, you might be considered an accessory to the crime."

I sat quietly while Hattie spoke. She appeared to be focusing on the negatives rather than the potential upside of a series of profitable sales. I told her as much. Hattie smiled. "I've been around a long time, John. It's easy to be lured into deals that seem like a sure thing, and perhaps this one might be. Mr. Moule seems to want to do business through you. We're certainly not the biggest gallery in town, and as you said, how did he choose you? Before you make any commitments to working with him, I think you need to do a bit of investigation. If he's legit, he won't hesitate to show you his bona fides, backing up his words with documentation."

Hattie was right. I knew that, but making and keeping the gallery profitable was a constant struggle. Part of me wanted to believe Moule was real, that this one opportunity would relieve my financial worries and possibly lead to bigger things. I needed Jenna's input. More than anyone else, she knew me and understood me. We met shortly after my release from prison, two souls trying to recover from the past, she from drugs and me from the loss of everything I once thought had meaning in my life. Jenna was born and raised in Claxton, a small former railroad town of scarcely more than 2,500 people located in the pine barren flatlands an hour west of Savannah. After getting out of rehab she had stayed clean and chose to return home to raise her young son away from the life in the city that had dragged her down.

As was our custom, we met at the McDonald's in Pembroke, another tiny village on the rail line halfway between Claxton and Savannah. Sitting outside, shielded by a red umbrella from the warm afternoon sunlight, I once again explained the situation with Moule. Jenna listened quietly. "The whole thing sounds really iffy, John," she said when I finished.

"How so?"

"It's something you want to do, I can sense that, but you're afraid of making some huge mistake, of screwing up and losing everything again." She was right. "I can't tell you what to do, or even give you advice this time. What did Jessica and Hattie say?"

"Like you," I said, "they seem suspicious of the situation, but they only urged me to be careful. I don't believe either one feels they are in a position to tell me exactly what to do, even if I had directly asked them to. But you and I have a different relationship. At this point in my life, you know me better than anyone. You know my—no, our—darkest secrets. I trust you. Tell me what you think I should do."

Jenna looked down, her long blonde hair covering her face as she jiggled the straw in her drink, considering how to reply. "Okay. Do this. Get—no, demand—more information, more documentation to be sure the guy is for real. Bank statements, maybe some sort of certificate from the experts who authenticated the painting—who was the artist again?"

"Rothko."

"Right, Rothko. And anything else you can find on this guy Moule. Google him. Have a discreet background check run. If all that is pure as the driven snow, then and only then would I move ahead."

"But what…?" I began.

"You were about to ask me what if he objected, or refused to give you financial references, right?"

I nodded.

"If he's honest, he won't hesitate one minute. He's in the business and I'm sure he knows there are lots of scammers out there. You'll simply be doing your due diligence." She stopped, waiting for me to reply.

"I'll sleep on it and make a decision tomorrow morning."

"Smart," Jenna said.

CHAPTER 5

I was at a loss about what to do. Neither Jessica nor Hattie nor
Jenna, the three people I thought I could trust the most, had
advised me to walk away from a deal with Moule, but each
cautioned me to be careful. I needed the income, but dealing
with a strange character engaged in what might be a shady business worried me. Trying to put things in perspective, I realized
that if we could reach some type of agreement—my acting as
Moule's agent to find and purchase investment-quality art—
we could take the relationship a step at a time. No deals until
the money was in my escrow account—that sort of thing. It
just might work; I'd have much to gain and little to lose if we
structured the agreement correctly, providing a way that would
allow me to bail any time the financial arrangements began to
falter, or if the situation made me suspicious. Practicing law for
years had honed my sense of detection of shysters and con men.
I vowed that the lure of money would not lull me into a sense
of complacency.

I called Moule the next morning and set up an appointment to meet him the following day at his house. He said he
would clear his schedule for several hours, agreeing to see me
at 10:00 a.m. A million-dollar deal would require a lot of planning and a deep understanding of the goals of each side. Mine,
of course, was to make a profit by offering my services as a
buyer's agent, taking a commission plus expenses for each sale.
I needed to more fully grasp Moule's objectives. Did he simply
want works of art with lasting value and whose sale price might
increase with time? Did he plan to display them or keep them
locked away in a vault somewhere? How did he intend to pay
for them? I presumed he knew that few, if any, sellers would

accept anything other than a cashier's check backed by either dollars or euros. Bitcoin and other such volatile digital currencies would not do. And I would need both personal and financial references, of course. Once we worked out the broad details, I would begin looking into his credentials and business dealings. I promised myself that if there was one moment of hesitation on his cooperation with a background check, I would politely end the conversation and walk out the door.

The next morning I decided to drive rather than walk, parking my car on East Gaston Street in front of Moule's house. I studied the structure for a moment before I climbed the steps and rang the bell. Its restoration, still gleamingly new, had been done with precision and meticulous attention to detail. Minor repairs to the brickwork, something that would have been necessary given the structure's age, were barely perceptible. Two small video cameras surveyed the front yard and driveway, while a third on the porch pointed at the front door. I presumed there were others. Moule answered the door promptly. "John, I'm glad you're here. I'm excited to get started on our adventure," he said, smiling broadly. "I sent the maid home for a few hours so we'll have the place to ourselves to talk. No need for prying eyes and ears."

We sat in the large room downstairs with its white walls and colorful canvases. After a few casual formalities Moule got right to the point. "I know we haven't discussed this, but I would be foolish if I didn't think the first thing you'd want to do is check to see if I'm for real, to see if someone who makes his living dealing in cryptocurrencies is not some sort of crook." He smiled and waited for my reply.

"Uh, yes, that is on my list—but please don't take it personally. If things progress, we may be dealing with some very expensive works. I think it's to both of our advantages to be sure of things before we get started. And of course, you will want to check out my background…"

"I already have," Moule said, interrupting me. "I did that before we met the other day. I know about your prison record—you got a raw deal there, by the way—and that you inherited the gallery from your grandmother. Your banker and a few others that I've talked with tell me you're honest, knowledgeable, and can be trusted. That's really all I need to know."

I was more than a little taken aback. Reaching over to a table to pick up a large folio, Moule continued, "On my end, I've put together this package of information on my background, my qualifications, my business, and most importantly my financial situation. I believe you'll find most of what you need in here, but I encourage you to have me checked out thoroughly. I'll be happy to answer any questions and introduce you to my bankers and other financial folks I deal with." He waited for a brief moment to see if I would reply, then said, "I hope this is helpful."

I tried not to act surprised, replying with a simple, "Thank you. I'm sure it will be," then tried to change the subject. "What I would like to do today is have you tell me as precisely as you can what you want me to do for you, and for my understanding, make it a little clearer just why you're doing this. Quality works of art, along with so many other—if I can use the word—'alternative' investments, can be very profitable. But I need to tell you before we get started that oftentimes they can't be quickly converted back to cash. Selling them for the highest price often takes time—many months sometimes. And if the economy hits one of its periodic recessions or other downturns, people are often hesitant to buy at all. You do understand that?"

Moule smiled, the look on his face suggesting I had just

said something completely obvious, as if I had reminded an airline pilot that planes can crash. "I know, and I know very well. It's part of the game. Maybe I didn't make myself clear the other day. I make my living by trading currencies. Few things can be more irregular, unpredictable, and subject to wide swings in value."

I smiled back and nodded. "Let's get started then." For the next two hours we went over his current art collection in detail. Most of his works were of good quality and style, but by unknown or lesser known artists. They were perfect for their current use—wall decoration—but had little value as short or long term investments. In his bedroom suite, the two Cora Dell Meadows works from the 1920s had excellent resale value, probably far more than he had paid for them. The work that resembled a Pollock had potential but needed to be verified. It was clearly of the right style, and the canvas appeared to be of the correct age. I told him I would see about getting a formal opinion from an expert on the artist. The most valuable piece, the Rothko, had been authenticated by a member of the staff of the National Gallery in Washington, DC, which holds the largest collection of the artist's work. "There are copies of the documentation for that in the folder I gave you," Moule said. I had brought along my digital camera and took a photo of each painting as we reviewed the works. In one of our earlier conversations, Moule said that he generally liked the genre of abstract expressionism, but I needed to review what hung on his walls to have a better feel for what he was willing to invest in. When choosing pieces to buy, I could be more efficient by focusing on paintings that I thought he would like.

Perhaps most importantly, I needed to know his plans for his investment. Why art? Why not other types of secure investments, or if he wanted something untraceable, concealable, portable, and valuable, why not gold or other precious metals? So I asked. Moule looked up briefly at the ceiling as if gathering his thoughts and then began, "I believe I told you I was into gaming when I was younger—video games, you know. Back in the day—which really hasn't been that long ago—there was Pac-Man and Tetris and Super Mario Brothers and the like, and then came more realistic games like Grand Theft Auto and others and Sony's PlayStation and high-resolution TVs that could almost make you think you were part of the action. Looking back, I got addicted to all these fantasy worlds, so much so that I began to prefer my digital life to reality." He paused and took a deep breath. "I'm no fool. The truth is that I didn't have a real life, just my video world. I can look in the mirror. I'm short. I'm bald. I'm fat. I'm not good with people, but hey, online I'm a hero, the guy who wins the game, who kills the dragon, who wins the love of the princess…" Moule's voice trailed off as I thought I saw the gleam of a tear in his eyes. He took another deep breath and continued, "Anyway, I came to my senses, enrolled in my community college, and just kept going. I put that life—the imaginary world of video games—behind me. One thing led to another and I got into the world of cryptocurrencies. And I'm good at it. I've been successful, or so they say. I've made lots of money…but …but I realized that that world is not real either. Bitcoin and the other cryptos are valuable because we get together and agree they are. They don't really exist. They are just digital fantasies in a weird sort of adult game called currency trading." Moule paused and dabbed at his eyes. "The paintings, though, they are real. They're beautiful, and I can touch them and feel the brushstrokes of their creators and…" He stopped suddenly. I said nothing, waiting for him to continue. For an awkward moment, the room was quiet. The yodeling wail of a police siren from the direction of Forsyth Park rose then faded into the distance. Moule said, "I'm sorry. I didn't mean to get started on all that and make a fool of myself."

"You didn't. We all have a history of sorts, sometimes painful…"

"I know," Moule said, looking up. "That's part of the reason I asked you to help me invest in art."

CHAPTER 6

I left Moule's house immensely encouraged. Not only had he been upfront in offering verification of his financial dealings, but I had also gained insight into who he was as well as his past and his hang-ups. I told him I would need a week or two to get up a representation agreement and craft a formal presentation showing him how I intended to proceed with my search for investment-grade works of art. He seemed quite happy with our meeting, and we parted ways on a positive note. Although I did not mention it, my primary task would be to check his references, both personal and financial.

Back at the gallery, the first call I made was to Phil Holloway, the attorney who defended me following Abraham Deign's attempt to frame me for the murder of his granddaughter. Holloway was a partner at Randolph, Holloway & Lamar, one of the better known law firms in the state. Because their primary practice revolved around criminal defense, they also had one of the best investigative teams in Savannah, just what I needed to follow up on Moule's past and present. I spent a few minutes explaining the situation to Holloway. "Sounds like you're jumping in with two feet, eh, John?" Holloway said. "That's great. You deserve some successes after all you've been through these past few years."

"Yeah, I'd like to think this relationship could be a winner for me business-wise, but I've got to be suspicious. It's almost too good of an opportunity."

"We can help," Holloway replied. "If you're free this afternoon, how about coming over to my office so we can get started straightaway? I'll get the investigators right on it."

I met with Holloway for more than an hour. Although I

initially thought I would ask his firm for just a criminal check on Moule, I realized after talking with him that they had the expertise and wherewithal to give me a complete profile on the man, his business, his background, and any criminal or civil actions that had been filed against him going back as far as I wanted. In short, they would be able to do all that I needed. It would be expensive, of course, but worth it in terms of speed and simplicity. Holloway said he would take it on as a special project. I gave him the go-ahead and passed on the folder of reference material that Moule had given me.

For my part, I began drafting a representation agreement. The standard gallery markup for an artist's work sold on consignment is one hundred percent; the artist and the gallery split the retail selling price of the painting equally. Since Moule had the potential to be the gallery's biggest customer, for works purchased on his behalf I proposed a commission of thirty percent above my purchase price, plus any personal expenses such as airfare, lodging, shipping, insurance and the like. Thinking of the alleged Pollock he had purchased, I would add extra charges if it became necessary to ascertain the authenticity or trace the provenance of the paintings, but these would be counted as expenses and would not be commissionable. There were multiple "indemnify and hold harmless" clauses designed to protect both parties. It took me three days and multiple drafts before I finally ended up with what I thought was a fair and workable agreement, in all seven single-spaced pages of mostly ten-point type. I printed out a copy and put it in my safe, holding it while I waited for Holloway's investigators to give me their report.

A week later I called Moule to reassure him that I was still working on things and would call him again as soon as I had everything in place. He seemed fine with that and ended the conversation with a pleasant "No rush."

Two weeks after my initial meeting with Phil Holloway, he called to say that his team had a preliminary report on one "Donald D'Entremont-Moule," deliberately pronouncing the name with a faux-French accent. "The first time you told me the guy's name I didn't say anything, but the thought crossed my mind that it had to be some kind of alias, a fake name or something. But no, my guys tell me he's for real. If you've got a few minutes to spare, we can go over their report now." I told him I would be at his office in fifteen minutes.

We met in Holloway's conference room. He handed Moule's folder back to me while he consulted a thick sheaf of documents in a spiral binder. "Here's the report," Holloway said. "You'll want to go over it in detail, of course, but let me hit the highlights." He opened the binder to the first page. "My guys traced Moule's history from the time he began his PhD program at Stanford up until the present. His background and education seem to be primarily in computer programming, with an emphasis on advanced mathematics and data management. About"—Holloway paused while he traced his finger down a page—"here it is—twelve years ago, he got involved in digital money, sort of getting in on the ground floor, as it were. He was employed with several start-ups until about five and a half years ago when he went out on his own as an independent consultant specializing in cryptocurrencies." Holloway looked up over his reading glasses. "I have no idea whatsoever about all that electronic money stuff, John, but I'm just repeating what we found." He looked back at the binder and continued. "Moule's had no run-ins with the law or any regulatory bodies that we could find. He holds all the right certifications and licenses—there's a list of them in here—and has had no complaints to organizations like the Better Business Bureau, or government agencies like the SEC—the Securities and Exchange Commission. Basically, he's got a clean record." Holloway watched me, as if trying to gauge my reaction.

"So far, so good," I said. "So good in fact that I'm waiting for the other shoe to drop."

"That's just it. There is no other shoe. The rest of this report," Holloway said, tapping the binder, "is financial stuff. Moule has money, lots of it in fact. The problem is that a lot of it's in the form of various cryptocurrencies. He has," Holloway said, again consulting the page in front of him, "what appears to be about $8,500,000 in cash and semi-liquid investments, but—and I had to ask to make sure there wasn't a mistake or a typo here—roughly $28,000,000 in digital currency, mainly in Bitcoin, Ethereum, and Solana—I hope I'm pronouncing those names correctly." He closed the binder and waited for my reply.

To say I was stunned would have been the understatement of the decade. "Wow," was all I could say, trying to buy a bit of time as the enormity of Holloway's report sank into my brain. "That's a lot…"

"I know." Holloway said. "What are you going to do?"

"I'm not sure. The first thing I want to do is read your report. And the second and third and fourth things after that will be to read it again."

"Then…?"

"If it all makes sense, I'll probably do business with him," I said.

I thanked Holloway and stumbled out of his office, half in a daze.

I spent many of my waking hours for the next three days reading and rereading the report prepared by Holloway's investigators. It was comprehensive, professional, and, so far as I could tell, complete. Moule had given permission in advance to his primary banker and broker, both of whom were interviewed for the record and both of whom provided documents to substantiate the figures Holloway had initially quoted to me. Moule was a rich man; there was no doubt about that. Despite whatever reservations or suspicions I might have, I could not objectively find a reason not to do business with him. On the morning of the fourth day, after a sleepless night spent tossing and turning in my bed, I called him to set up an appointment.

Moule seemed pleased at my call but said he was tied up the remainder of the day and would be out of town the next. He asked if we could meet the following day, a Saturday. "The markets will be closed and the maid has the weekend off anyway, so we won't be disturbed," he said. "Will 2 p.m. work for you?"

"Sure," I said, and scratched the date on my calendar highlighted by a star. Unusually nervous, I spent several hours on Friday in my gallery office with the door closed, practicing how I wanted to approach Moule with the agreement.

Toward the middle of the afternoon Jessica knocked on my door and asked if she could come in. "Are you sure you're all right?" she asked. "You haven't been yourself lately, and when I hear you shut up in here talking to yourself, I just can't help but worry."

For the first time in more than a week, I laughed. She knew I was negotiating with Moule, but I had not shared any details with her. "I'm fine," I said, smiling. "I had Moule checked out. I believe he's legit. I'm meeting with him tomorrow to sign a representation agreement. If it all works out like I hope it will, the gallery will be in great shape—no, *we'll* be in great shape. Maybe we can afford that raise you've been wanting."

At the mention of a raise, Jessica beamed. "Go for it then," she said, returning to her desk with a grin.

Promptly at 1:58 p.m. the next afternoon I parked my car in front of Moule's house, climbed the steps, took a deep breath while mentally crossing my fingers, and pressed the bell button. I waited. A minute passed, then two. I rang the bell again, thinking that perhaps Moule had not heard it, or was taking a nap, or had stepped out into his backyard. Five minutes passed. I grasped the oversized brass door knocker and sharply rapped it three times against the plate on the door. Again, nothing. Now worried, I pulled out my cell phone and dialed Moule's office number, the only one I had for him. After a brief pause, I could discern the distant ringing of a phone somewhere deep inside the house. With no answer, I pressed the end button. The ringing stopped. It was now more than ten minutes after the hour. Moule must have forgotten, I said to myself. No doubt he'll call with his apologies and all will be well. I turned to walk back to my car, but at the last minute decided to try the door handle. To my surprise, it turned easily, opening the door a small crack. I peeked inside.

The lights in the large downstairs room were on, the paintings illuminated by the overhead spotlights. All was quiet. I called out, "Don?" No response. I called again, louder this time, "Don? Hey, this is John O'Toole. I'm here for our two o'clock meeting." Still no reply. I let myself in and shut the door behind me. The large room was empty. The powder room door under the stairway was open, the light inside off. I pushed open the kitchen door behind the dining area. It, too, was empty and provided a clear view of the backyard through the rear windows. Moule was nowhere to be seen.

I took out my cell phone, considering calling 911, but realized I could be accused of illegally entering a private home, appointment or not. I walked over to the base of the stairs and called Moule's name. Again, no answer. Slowly and cautiously I began climbing the steps, each creaking loudly under my feet. At the top, I turned to the right toward Moule's workspace. The door was open, the computer screens glowing in the dimness, but the room was otherwise empty.

Moule's bedroom suite was toward the back of the house. The door was closed. I cracked it open just a hair and called out Moule's name. There was no answer. I could see the paintings on the wall, including the one he thought was the work of Pollock. I opened the door wider and could now see the king-sized bed against the far wall. There, squarely in the middle of the bed, Moule lay propped up on pillows against the headboard. Above his head, where the Rothko hung, the wall appeared to have been repainted with some sort of large red irregular Rorschach blot. It was then that I saw the gun and recognized the pattern on the wall as one made by blood and brains.

CHAPTER 7

I dialed 911. Five rings—an eternity—then a click and an expressionless female voice saying, "911: What's your emergency?"

"I…I, uh…" I realized I had trouble speaking. "I'm calling to, uh, report a shooting. I think the police need to…"

"Was anyone injured?" the voice asked.

"Yes. He appears to be dead."

The tone of the voice at the other end of the line immediately changed, peppering me with questions: "What is your name? What is your exact location? Is there only one victim? Is the shooter still in the area? Was this an accident, or does it appear to be a criminal act? Besides the police, do we need to send an ambulance and EMTs?" I gave her my name and Moule's address. I told her that I had just discovered the body, that I had not seen anyone else and didn't know the circumstances of the shooting. I said I would wait outside on the street to meet the police.

The first patrol car arrived within three minutes, followed rapidly by another, their vehicles blocking my car parked in front of Moule's house. The first officer leapt out of his vehicle, hand on gun, and, like the 911 operator, shot off a quick series of queries: "Are you O'Toole?" I nodded. "Did this shooting just happen? Where is the shooter? Where is the victim?" I briefly explained the situation, that I had a 2:00 p.m. appointment with Mr. Moule, but when he didn't answer the door I let myself in and found his body in an upstairs bedroom. "So you just entered the house, not knowing if anyone was home?" the cop asked.

"I said I had an appointment. No one answered the door.

35

It was unlocked, so…?" My voice trailed off as I tried to explain.

The policeman frowned, looked at the other cop, and gestured with his head toward Moule's front door. Turning back to me he said, "You stay right here. Do not try to leave. We'll have questions." With that, both disappeared into the house. Ten minutes passed. A third and fourth patrol car arrived, each with two officers who blocked off both ends of the street with yellow crime scene tape before joining the others inside. I leaned against the fender of my car as fifteen more minutes went by. I could see small crowds of curious onlookers gathering at either end of the police cordon. Two more police vehicles arrived, one a nondescript white Tahoe with a local government tag, followed shortly by an older Crown Victoria with a Chatham County logo emblazoned on both doors below the word "Coroner." Several officers took up crowd control duty while others, including two men in suits, entered Moule's house. I thought I recognized at least one of them.

Shortly before 2:45, the same two men emerged from Moule's front door, walking with firm deliberation in my direction. I had been correct; the man in the lead was Senior Detective Roderick Q. Labonsky of the Savannah metro police. He sized me up a moment before speaking. "Mr. O'Toole, why do we have to keep meeting like this?" Labonsky's voice was laced with sarcasm. I did not respond. He had been the lead Savannah detective in the investigation of the kidnapping and murder of Lucy Deign and had arrested me as the prime suspect. His ego, and no doubt his career, had suffered when the case fell apart and I was exonerated. "They say you found the deceased's body," Labonsky continued. "Tell me about it."

I briefly explained that Moule had planned to hire me to help him purchase works of art for investment purposes. Other than checking on his business and financial background, I knew little or nothing about his personal life, including his friends and associates.

"So you had no hint of any reason why he might want to commit suicide?"

The word took me by surprise. "Suicide?" The thought that Moule's death was self-inflicted had never entered my mind. "No, not at all. That'd be the last thing I'd think of. He seemed happy, and was excited about purchasing art for his collection. Materially, he had everything anyone could want— he was beyond wealthy, he was rich…"

"Terminally rich, it would appear," Labonsky said, again with a hint of sarcasm.

"What makes you think he killed himself?" I asked. Immediately after discovering Moule's body I had walked outside to call 911. I hadn't taken time to look about the room, but presumed they had found a note or some other clue.

"Well, someone put the gun in Moule's mouth and pulled the trigger. The gun's there on the bed next to his right hand, and his brains are all over the wall behind him. Seems pretty obvious." The second man in a suit, whom Labonsky had not bothered to introduce, nodded in agreement. "But the CSI crew will be here shortly to work the scene and gather evidence, just to be sure." He glanced over my shoulder. "Oh, here they are now." A large panel truck was just clearing the police barrier and easing its way down the street. "I'm going back inside to help gather evidence and take photos. Detective Marsh here is going to take your statement." Labonsky turned to greet the CSI truck but, apparently having a second thought, looked back to me and said, "Just in case things don't sort out like I think they will, we may need to interview you in more detail downtown." He paused. "Like before, remember?"

Once again I went over my relationship with Moule, as limited as it had been, while the detective scribbled notes on a spiral pad. Marsh asked a few questions, took my contact information, and said they would be in touch, if necessary. I had the impression that the issue of Moule's cause of death had been decided, that most of what was being done at the moment were mere formalities. Marsh, whose first name was Pete, radioed one of the first two officers who had arrived on the scene and had him move his patrol car so I could drive out. Heading west toward Forsyth Park, I realized that several of the curiosity seekers who had gathered just beyond the police line were reporters and journalists. The officers blocking my exit had been advised that I was leaving and moved their white and orange barricades as I approached. Just beyond, however, my car was mobbed by half a dozen microphone and camera-wielding reporters who tapped on my window yelling, "Can you tell us what's going on in there? What's your connection? Can you give us a statement?" or something similar. I waved briefly but otherwise ignored them, trying to disappear by slipping into the Drayton Street traffic.

The last weeks could only be described as bizarre. There had been highs and lows and hope and uncertainty. The prospect of some financial security had been dangled in front of my eyes, then jerked away with Moule's suicide. And what would become of Moule's fortune? He had never mentioned a family, or for that matter anyone else, during our several conversations. What would happen to his art collection? Most of it was pretty routine and not of great value, but the work by Mark Rothko was something.... And then I realized—the Rothko hung directly over Moule's bed. It would have been covered with blood and other debris if the blast from the gun didn't destroy it. I didn't remember seeing it, but then I didn't dwell on the horror and gore of the whole scene. The Rothko was lost, for sure.

I drove home to my carriage house, parked my car in the alleyway, and for the first time in nearly five years poured myself a drink of whiskey. I waited ten minutes and called Phil Holloway.

CHAPTER 8

Holloway listened quietly as I told him what had happened starting with my arrival at Moule's house at 2:00 p.m., acknowledging my account with a periodic "Uh-huh." When I stopped to catch my breath, there was silence on the other end of the line, then, "You're kidding, right? I hope you're making all this up."

"No."

"Shit," Holloway said, followed by another long pause. "And Labonsky's handling the case? How ironic can you get? It's a sad situation, for sure… But why would Moule want to kill himself? At least you're not a suspect this time."

"I hope not," I said. "Labonsky said it was an obvious case of suicide, but he called in the crime scene crew just the same."

"That's got to be routine," Holloway said.

"Yeah, you'd think so." We were silent for a moment, both in thought. "But like you said," I continued, "why would Moule want to kill himself? For sure, we don't know much about him, but from what he said to me he seemed to have his demons under control, he was apparently successful in business and unbelievably wealthy, he was looking forward to expanding his art collection… Why?"

"My guys just ran a thorough background check on him, so that tends to rule out a lot of business and financial reasons," Holloway said. "It could be something deeply personal that we don't know about. I'd venture that unless the CSI people find a suicide note or something like that, we'll probably never know. Those sort of things happen. Let me know if you hear anything." We talked a few more minutes before hanging up. I felt somewhat better, but deep inside I harbored a vague sense of unease.

The weekend passed quietly. The Sunday paper and the online news feeds carried no mention of Moule's death, with the same on Monday and Tuesday mornings. I spoke with Jessica, Hattie, and Jenna, filling them in on what happened. Jessica responded with, "It's sad, but I'm not surprised. He was just too weird." She didn't mention the promised raise, but I could read her disappointment in the look on her face. Hattie said she was sorry to hear the news as well, but equally disappointed at the loss of a potential business windfall. Jenna's reaction was more nuanced, expressing dismay at Moule's suicide but greater concern about what it might mean for me or my reputation, "even though you had nothing to do with his death." By Tuesday afternoon, seventy-two hours after the discovery of Moule's body, the free-floating anxiety that had caused me three sleepless nights seemed to be waning. It bothered me a bit that there had been a crowd of reporters near Moule's house on Saturday, yet so far as I had seen, there was nothing in the news. Probably the fact that his death was a suicide had lessened its news value. Whatever the cause, no news appeared to be good news from my perspective.

We were just about to close the gallery for the day on Tuesday afternoon when my cell phone rang. I didn't recognize the number but decided to answer it anyway. "Mr. O'Toole," a familiar voice said. "This is Detective Labonsky. We'd like to speak with you here at headquarters tomorrow morning. Can you meet us sometime fairly early, say 9:30 or 10:00?"

A pit seemed to open in my chest, and for a moment I felt lightheaded. "Uh, yes, sure. I take it this is about Moule?"

"Yeah, we'll go over the details tomorrow when we talk. It's kinda complicated."

"Should I bring my lawyer?" I asked, trying to sound

nonchalant.

"Not unless you're feeling guilty about something," Labonsky fired back. The detective said he didn't want to discuss any details over the phone, leaving me to anticipate a fourth night of worry. We agreed to meet at 10:00 a.m. at the Savannah police headquarters complex on the corner of Habersham Street and Oglethorpe Avenue, a less than ten-minute walk from my gallery. I hung up and called Phil Holloway.

"I wonder what that means," Holloway said. "Labonsky remembered you, so maybe he just wants to rattle your cage, get you upset and let you stew overnight and then tell you he wanted to give you some routine follow-up. We made him look like a fool when he was giving testimony in the Deign case. He's probably salivating at the chance to repay the favor."

"Do you think you need to be there with me?"

"John, you're an attorney for god's sake," Holloway said, his voice forceful. "You know how the system works. Calm down. If you show up for a routine briefing accompanied by a criminal defense attorney, especially one who really pissed off the lead detective in the case, it's just going to make matters a lot worse. You haven't done anything. There's nothing they can charge you with. So relax. Wear some loose shoes. Go see Labonsky, listen to what he has to say. If things get tight, just don't say anything. You know the drill. I shouldn't have to tell you all this."

I did know the drill. And I knew Holloway was right. "Okay," I said. "It sounds like I'm looking for someone to hold my hand. I guess I am."

"You've survived worse. Call me after your meeting tomorrow." With that the line went dead.

Wednesday dawned overcast and dreary, perhaps a normal spring day for April on the Georgia coast, but similar to my mood and state of mind. I did not know what to expect from my meeting with Labonsky. Despite a chance of rain, I chose to walk to police headquarters, housed in a nineteenth century brick building next to the city's original cemetery dating from Georgia's colonial days in the mid-eighteenth century. Arriving a few minutes early, I was ushered into a small conference room where the detectives, Labonsky and Marsh, plus two other individuals awaited me. Labonsky acted as the host, introducing the other two as crime lab technicians. A small sheaf of documents lay in a neat pile on the table before him.

"Mr. O'Toole, I asked you to come down today to go over some unexpected findings at the scene of Donald Moule's death the other day," Labonsky said. "First, let me say my initial impression was evidently in error. That happens occasionally in criminal investigations, as you may remember." He paused briefly, looking to see if I caught his veiled reference to our shared history. My expression did not change. "Given the scene we found in the victim's bedroom, we logically assumed he committed suicide. On further examination by our crime lab techs, however, it appears that scene may have been staged. I will let Mr. Register go over the details with you." Labonsky motioned toward one of the techs. I tried to remain calm but could not keep my heart from pounding on hearing Labonsky's reference to "criminal investigations" and to Moule as a "victim."

Register began, "Mr. O'Toole, you discovered the victim's body, so I'll try to limit what I say to findings that surprised us and changed what appeared to be a death due to suicide to what seems to be a case of homicide—murder, if you will." Out of the corner of my eye I saw Labonsky and Marsh watching me intently, attempting to understand what was going through my mind based on these revelations. "There are two very important findings," Register continued. "First, Moule did not fire the bullet that caused the massive gaping exit wound just above his occiput—that's the back of his head, if the term is not familiar to you." He slid a large color photograph across the table. I felt nauseous at the sight. "Although the gun found near his hand had been fired, there was no powder residue on either Moule's right or left hand, findings that would be necessary if he himself had pulled the trigger. Here are some other photos if you'd like to see them." I shook my head and pushed them away. "We were able to recover an intact .357 magnum hollow-point bullet from the wall behind the deceased. It was badly deformed, but we feel confident it was in fact fired by that pistol and was the cause of Mr. Moule's death. We tried to trace the serial number of the gun, but we hit a dead end. It was evidently in circulation before the era of strict gun registration laws. Any questions thus far?"

I shook my head.

"The other finding of significance was the toxicology report on the victim's blood. To our surprise, we found significant levels of fentanyl. I don't know if you've heard of fentanyl, but it's become a commonly abused drug these days. It's a synthetic opioid, in the same general class as heroin, but can be taken by mouth instead of injected or smoked. Depending on how it's supplied, it can be up to a hundred times more powerful than morphine. We know Moule was alive when he was shot, or at least that his heart was still beating by the amount of blood around his body. It's speculation, of course, but it's possible that he was drugged, either covertly or against his will, and after he was unconscious, someone moved him to his bedroom and set up the scene to look like a suicide." The crime lab tech stopped, waiting for my response.

"Damn," I said. "So you're saying that it appears he was

murdered?"

"That's for the coroner to officially decide, but yeah, it looks that way," Labonsky replied, now back in charge.

"So why am I here?" I asked.

"We thought you'd want to know."

"Okay." Then I remembered. "But there were cameras—I saw a couple on the front of the house and one pointed toward the door—"

"We know," Labonsky said, interrupting me.

"What do *they* show?" I asked.

Labonsky seemed to be gathering his words before replying. "That information is confidential at this point. You see, Mr. O'Toole, we're still in the early stages of our investigation. We're looking at everything and everyone that might have had a motive or opportunity to do harm to Moule. You seem to have been working closely with him for a few weeks. We know that you found out he was a very wealthy man. And since you've had financial troubles in the past, it's only natural—"

"No!" I said, slamming my fist on the table. "I was working on a representation deal with Moule, but we had not reached any…"

Labonsky held his hand up, stopping me mid-sentence. "Let me show you one more photo. Perhaps you can give us some help in interpreting what we've found." He motioned to Register, who slid a large color photograph across the table to me. It appeared to be a thin rectangular object wrapped in brown kraft paper. "Do you recognize this? Perhaps you saw it propped against the wall in Moule's bedroom?"

"No," I said. "What is it?"

"Look at the upper right-hand corner there." I could barely make out something written on the brown paper. "Larry, show Mr. O'Toole the blowup," Labonsky directed.

Register slid another photo across the table. The words "To John O'Toole, with Appreciation," were written with a marker on the paper in a bold flowing script. Just below, it was signed in similar script, "Don Moule."

I frowned, confused. "What is this? I've never seen it before."

"Really?" Labonsky asked, his voice hinting at incredulity. "Well, let me show you." He motioned to Register who slid a third photo to me. In this one, the paper had been peeled back to reveal a medium-sized painting with irregular orange and red rectangles painted on a deep blue background. Labonsky saw the look on my face. "Apparently Moule wanted you to have it. I'm not sure why—it looks kinda amateurish to me. But they tell me it's by some guy named Rothko. I've never heard of him. Maybe you have. *Now* do you know anything about it?"

CHAPTER 9

I honestly believed the Rothko painting had been destroyed. The fact that it had not and, more bizarrely, the fact that Moule apparently intended to give it to me as a gift defied any reasonable explanation I could think of. I explained that to Labonsky and Marsh, both of whom appeared skeptical. "So that's a valuable painting?" Labonsky asked.

"Very much so, assuming it's real," I said.

"Why wouldn't it be? And what do you think it's worth?"

"There's a lot of counterfeit art out there," I begin, deliberately not mentioning that Moule had given me authentication documents from the National Gallery. "And the only real way to know its worth is to put it up for auction. I saw it hanging over the head of Moule's bed when he gave me a tour of his house. I assumed it had been pretty much destroyed with the"—I searched for the right word—"the mess."

Then something occurred to me. "But I went to his house on Saturday to sign an agreement," I said. "If things worked out, Moule was going to owe me a considerable sum in commissions. Maybe he was planning to offer the painting as collateral, or as a retainer against future commissions." The words sounded stupid as soon as they left my lips. From the looks on their faces, Labonsky and Marsh appeared unconvinced.

"Well," Labonsky said, "this has now turned into a murder investigation, and we've got a long way to go. Are you sure you don't know more about Moule than you're telling us? About his family, his next-of-kin, that kind of thing? Right now his body's in a cooler at the city morgue. We don't know who to notify."

"No, I'm sorry, I don't. This was strictly a new business

relationship."

"One that didn't work out, eh?" Labonsky said with a sardonic smile.

"I know he thinks I'm lying, or at the least, holding back something I know." I was back in Phil Holloway's conference room, nursing a cup of black coffee as I tried to explain the events of my morning visit to police headquarters.

"But look at it from Labonsky's viewpoint," Holloway countered. "You might think the same way if you were in his position. Moule was a loner. Most, if not all, of his business contacts would have been handled online. We haven't heard of any friends or relatives—I never met him, but from what you've said he doesn't strike me as the country club type, or the sort of guy who joins a Wednesday night bowling league. The connections are there, for sure, we just need to find them."

I looked up from my coffee. "We...?"

"Well, it's 'we' if they somehow try to drag you into this." Holloway paused. "But you've done nothing illegal, immoral, or unethical. There's no way in hell this is going to involve you beyond what's happened so far." He paused again, evidently thinking. "How about we get proactive with the police? Show them the financial and business information Moule gave you when you were running his background and references? It'll make you look helpful and eager to get things settled."

It was an excellent thought. We tossed the idea back and forth for a few minutes, deciding that I should personally deliver Moule's original folder of documents and references directly to the police, showing that I was trying to offer something that might assist them in their investigation. "We don't want to give them the background report my guys prepared," Holloway said. "If we did, and we somehow end up in court later, a good attorney for the other side might argue that we had already waived attorney-client privilege. That wouldn't be good."

"How can we—the police or us or anyone—explain why Moule apparently wanted to give me the Rothko painting?" I asked. "They don't know its real value, and as I said, I didn't tell them about its documentation from the National Gallery."

"I think we should just hold back on that. If the cops get the idea that you knew it was an original and worth a bunch, they might try to cook up some crazy scenario that Moule's murder was part of a plot you came up with to get your hands on it."

"Okay," I said. "So we offer them the folder and my co-operation?"

"To a point," Holloway said. "Just to a point. Those guys get paid to put a check mark by crimes solved. Anyone remotely connected, including you, can become the deer in their headlights."

I left Holloway's office feeling somewhat relieved. He was confident and reassuring, but his involvement was entirely tangential. I still couldn't suppress a vague sense of uncertainty. It suddenly hit me that I needed to get all of this out of my mind, take a few days off and try to relax. I called Jenna, who was still at work. "How about joining me this weekend somewhere?"

"Somewhere? And just where is somewhere?" I could imagine her smiling at the other end of the line.

"You name it. I was thinking maybe a B&B down the coast for a couple of nights. Just me and you and a little beach time. It's a little early for the summer crowds, so we could—"

"I'll call you back," Jenna said, ending the call with a click.

Ten minutes later my phone rang again. "I'm yours for the weekend. I had to make some arrangements for Conner, but that's done." She had asked her parents to watch her son and gotten permission to leave work a bit early. "So, want to pick me up, or shall I meet you somewhere?"

"I'll pick you up," I said. "Four o'clock, Friday afternoon." I smiled, feeling better for a change. I called Holloway and said I would drop off Moule's folder at police headquarters on my way out of town that afternoon. With that behind me, and the promise of Jenna's company to warm my soul, I could relax and forget the world for a few days.

Labonsky seemed both surprised and pleased when I called him to say I would be bringing by some financial reference material on Moule. "We appreciate your help, of course," he said, sounding quite genuine this time. I explained that I would give him the personal and financial records that Moule originally gave to me. I assured him we had checked Moule out and all seemed to be above board and in order. Labonsky said he would do the same and let me know if anything new came up. I delivered the material at mid-afternoon on Friday, then left for Claxton to pick up Jenna.

It was, in a few words, a delightful weekend. We stayed in a small bed and breakfast near the waterfront in Darien, a tiny eighteenth century town and former seaport some fifty miles south of Savannah. Despite the near-perfect weather, we spent hours indoors, reveling in each other's company. On Saturday, we took the ferry to nearby Sapelo Island, climbing to the top of the lighthouse to watch the sun sink into the western horizon. At night we dined on fresh-caught seafood, found endless things to talk about, and laughed at silly jokes. After I finally dropped Jenna off at her house late Sunday afternoon, I realized for the first time in a long while that I felt happy. The whole thing with Moule had faded into the background. Holloway was right. I had done nothing untoward, and therefore had nothing to worry about. For some reason, I remembered my turbulent childhood and my grandmother saying, "This too shall pass." I smiled.

CHAPTER 10

Two weeks went by, then three. I heard nothing from the police, and as before I found nothing about Moule's death in the newspapers or online. Out of curiosity, I rode past his house on East Gaston Street. Tattered yellow crime scene tape still blocked entry to the front porch. An orange placard whose words I couldn't make out was affixed to the front door. With the warmer weather and the beginning of summer, throngs of tourists once again crowded Savannah's streets. Art sales picked up significantly; June seemed likely to be a very profitable month. I was seeing Jenna at least once a week. She had given up her part-time job, having been awarded the position of assistant human resources manager, together with a significant raise, at the manufacturing firm where she worked.

On a Wednesday toward the end of the month, Detective Labonsky called. "Sorry I haven't been in touch," he began. "We've been working pretty hard on the Moule case." He seemed to hesitate a moment before continuing. "A few things have come up—I guess I should say we've found some things that are worrisome. We'd like to meet with you again to get your take on the situation."

"What sort of things?" I could feel my heart beating in my chest.

"It's complicated, and I'll need to fill you in on our investigation to let you know how we got where we are. But let me be clear—none of what we've found directly involves you. We've discussed it and think maybe your input will be helpful." I imagined that I could feel my heart rate slowing. "Anyway," Labonsky continued, "would you mind coming down to headquarters tomorrow or Friday? Several people will be involved, and it's easier for you to come to us than vice versa."

"Sure, I'm free tomorrow. What time?" I asked, relieved.

"Ten a.m. okay?" I said it was. "Good, we'll see you then," Labonsky said, adding, "Oh, if you'd like to bring your attorney, that would be fine. The more of us looking at the problem, the more likely we'll find a solution." The pounding in my chest returned, this time with a vengeance.

I called Holloway. He immediately agreed to accompany me as a client and as a friend, but mostly out of curiosity. "I can't imagine any great revelations. They're probably stuck and want to put a little pressure on you to see if they can squeeze out something you forgot to tell them. Let's go and see what they have to say." He sounded relaxed. I was still worried.

Just before ten o'clock the following morning, we were ushered into the same conference room at police headquarters. Labonsky and Marsh awaited us as before, with two new faces this time, one younger and one older. I introduced Holloway to the group. Labonsky's face hardened for a brief moment, but he shook his hand cordially, as did the other three. The younger of the two unknowns was introduced as Detective Sergeant Sellers and the older as Agent James Hasty of the FBI's Criminal Investigative Division. My heart began to pound again. We sat down while Labonsky took the lead. "Well, we've made some progress on the Moule investigation, but we've sort of hit a wall. That's why I asked you to come back today, John." This was the first time he had addressed me by my given name. "And Mr. Holloway, I'm glad you could be here. We discovered in the course of our investigation that your firm had also been involved. I believe what we've found will give you some valuable feedback.

"I won't belabor the point," Labonsky continued, "but as you know this started with a fairly routine investigation of what appeared to be the suicide of a middle-aged man. Rather soon after the start, we discovered that it was an apparent case of murder, with the crime scene staged to appear as if Moule had shot himself. There was no note or other indication that he had planned to end his life, and when we found his hands had no powder residue and took a closer look at the whole situation, the case became even more complicated. I want to go over what we've discovered and what we now know and see if perhaps either of you can add anything that might be of help." Labonsky paused, looking squarely at me and then at Holloway.

"First," he continued, "we started with a routine background check, and since it appeared that the victim was in the financial business, we also looked at that aspect of his life. The material that you gave us, John, made our job a lot easier. The strange thing, though, when we contacted the references that Moule had provided to you, we found that just one day before he was killed, he had moved most of his assets elsewhere. I'll tell you more about that in a minute. Now here we start running into an inconsistency. When we first interviewed you that Saturday after you discovered Moule's body, you said that you had called him a couple of days earlier to arrange a meeting. According to our notes, you said that Moule told you he had to be out of town the next day, which would have been a Friday. He told you he could meet the following day, which is when he was killed."

Labonsky looked down at a document on top of the pile of papers in front of him. "Well, when we called his financial people, it seems that he was on the phone the entire day Friday arranging the transfer of the majority of his assets to a division of Swissbanc, an international banking firm chartered in the Cayman Islands. The summary details of all that are here in these documents." He held up a thin folder. "This finding concerned us, of course, and we sought help from the FBI." He looked at Agent Hasty, who nodded.

Hasty said, "Let me add here—in case it's not obvious—that once Moule's funds were transferred to Swissbanc, we lost our ability to monitor them. The banking authorities in the Cayman Islands are not known for their willingness to work with international law enforcement. Once the assets are there, it's like they've disappeared into a black hole."

"There's more to that aspect," Labonsky said. "The second thing we did was to try to look into Moule's background. I believe your people did the same thing and got a clean slate, Mr. Holloway, but I suspect they didn't dig far enough because if they had, neither of you would be sitting here today. On our own, and subsequently with the help of the feds, we tried to trace Moule's life back as far as we could timewise. The first red flag came when we found that Moule applied for and was assigned a Social Security number twenty-six years ago, when he would have been twenty years old, assuming the date of birth we have is correct. Before that, we cannot find any public records in the name of Donald D'Entremont-Moule." Looking again at me, Labonsky added, "You said he told you he had moved to Savannah from Albuquerque. We searched the records in that city, for New Mexico and the adjacent states of the southwest, and found nothing. We were able to confirm that someone named Donald Dentremont Moule—no apostrophe or hyphen in that name, though—did attend a local community college in Salinas, California, and subsequently went on to earn a PhD from Stanford. The problem is, this person, who I presume is our deceased, started college at age twenty, a few months after the Social Security number was issued in his name." Turning toward the FBI agent, Labonsky said, "Do you want to comment here, Jim?"

"I don't really have a lot to add to what you've said thus far," Hasty said. "The federal government has been keeping digitized records organized in vast databases for decades. Sometimes we miss something, but that's pretty rare, especially with a name like Donald D'Entremont-Moule. The obvious conclusion is that he was someone else a couple of decades ago and changed his name to Moule. Records of name changes are maintained on a state and sometimes local level, and although they usually show up sooner or later in federal data, there's no practical way to track down every name change. From my perspective, the main concern of the federal government in this case is a murder that occurred in close association with large sums of money being moved offshore."

During all of this Holloway and I had sat transfixed, overwhelmed by the dramatic twists in the case. He spoke first. "It's hard to know what to say, where to start…"

"There's more," Labonsky said, holding up his palm. "The third thing is Moule's records, the files and documents he kept in the office at his house. He was a loner from all that we've seen, and we know he did most of his trading of stocks and bonds, plus his buying and selling or whatever you do with these cryptocurrency things, from his home. So we figured he'd keep records there that would shed some light on the situation." Labonsky took a deep breath. "But like nearly everything else in this case, we keep running into brick walls. In this situation, it was what we *didn't* find that's suspicious. Everything Moule did was digital—essentially no paper records. We had our IT guys look at his computers and their drives and the like. With one exception, everything was on the up-and-up. The one thing that seemed out of place was a laptop sitting on Moule's primary desk. It was not connected to anything: no ethernet cable, the Wi-Fi and Bluetooth turned off. What was weird—and my guys pointed this out to me—is there were no flash drives, no SSDs, no offline storage anywhere to be found in the entire house. They did find a receipt from where Moule had ordered and received two one-terabyte solid state drives from Amazon, but they were nowhere to be found. I would have never thought of that, but to them it stood out like a dead skunk at a picnic. If it's not connected to the net, that's for a reason, they tell me. It's confidential, or secret or private or whatever. We believe that either Moule, or whoever killed him, must have taken the drives."

The detective waited for reactions, but when we remained silent he shuffled through the papers in front of him and extracted a blowup of a photo. "John," he said, "you asked about the video cameras. There were a total of seven of them at Moule's house, three in the front that I believe you saw, and four more elsewhere. All of them were outside; there were no video cameras or other recording equipment inside that we could find. We did find the DVR, however, the digital video recorder. It was in the closet under the stairs together with the electronics for the alarm system. When our guys tried to recover the video on its hard drive, we discovered that it had been wiped clean and then restarted at 12:32 p.m. on the day of Moule's death. The first thing of importance you see on the video is you, John, standing on his front porch, ringing the bell and trying to decide whether to stay or go."

"What about other videos?" I asked. "I'm sure someone in the neighborhood has cameras, or video doorbells, or—"

"We thought about that. There was only one that captured anything of interest." Labonsky passed the photo over to Phil and me. "This is from the doorbell camera of the house directly across the street. It's a screenshot from about a minute and a half of video that begins at roughly 9:30 a.m. Two figures can be seen approaching Moule's house from the east, walking casually, not in a hurry. They seem to know exactly where they're going, as they don't hesitate but turn straight onto Moule's front walk and then up to his door. They ring the bell, and someone who pretty clearly seems to be Moule opens the door, greets them briefly, then lets them in. They were on the porch for only about forty-five seconds. The photo I just handed you shows his visitors. As you can see, it's going to be hard to identify anyone based on the video or that image alone."

Holloway and I studied the grainy image. It had been enlarged and printed in an eleven-by-fourteen-inch format. Two figures, one taller and one shorter, were dressed nondescriptly. Both wore baseball caps and sunglasses. Both had longer hair, one taller figure dark-headed, the shorter figure blonde. "It's hard to say anything about identity from this photo," Holloway commented.

"Or the video, for that matter," Labonsky added. "There is one thing, though. We think the shorter figure is female. There's nothing that absolutely points at that—you can't make out any breasts, for example. But the way they walked... We've had a couple of dozen people look at it, and the consensus is that Moule was visited by a man and a woman. Comparing heights to the doorframe, by the way, the shorter of the two appears to be about five-five or five-six inches in height. The taller is about five-eleven or six feet." Holloway and I passed the photo back and forth several times.

"Fingerprints...?" Holloway began.

"We checked of course," Labonsky said, cutting him off. "Just prints of Moule and his maid, the woman who worked there cleaning and cooking during the week. Moule had told her to take the day off on that Friday, by the way." He paused.

"Oh, and I almost forgot: Moule's video security system is programmable as to recording times. His two visitors were gone when it started back collecting video about an hour and a half before you showed up. It appears that they'd set it to start recording at about 12:30 p.m. We didn't catch any useful images of them leaving on any other of the neighborhood video cameras."

"So where do things stand now?" Holloway asked. "How do we come in? Or how can we be of help?"

Labonsky looked at Hasty, the FBI agent, who nodded. "We thought we should make you aware of the situation, for what that's worth. We have the murder victim, the late Mr. Moule, a man with an unknown if not mysterious background. He seems to have approached you, John, wanting to transact some business, to buy some art. You investigate him and discover that he has millions of dollars in various accounts. Then he ends up dead under very suspicious circumstances."

"So how does that involve us?" Holloway asked.

Labonsky glanced quickly again at Hasty, then asked, "How tall are you, Mr. Holloway? And you, Mr. O'Toole?"

CHAPTER 11

"Bastards!"

Holloway and I were sitting in my car parked on the street outside of Savannah police headquarters. I knew him well enough to know he was furious. His years as a courtroom criminal defense attorney had taught him to hide his emotions and any body language that might betray them. Now, in the privacy of the vehicle, he exploded. Reaching up to loosen his tie, he continued. "If they are so convinced that we're hiding something—or worse, part of some scheme to get our hands on Moule's money—why the hell don't they just confront us?"

"Two things," I said. "I agree with the idea that the cops—Labonsky at least—thinks that I'm dirty, and probably both of us because it was your guys who found out how much cash Moule was sitting on. What they're doing is so damned obvious, asking for our input and assistance and then springing the idea that it may have been one of us who was directly involved in his murder." I was angry as well. "But the other thing is this: Why didn't they just come right out and say it, tell us we're 'persons of interest'? That they're going to get some judge to sign a search warrant and—"

"I'll tell you why," Holloway interjected. "They've probably already gotten a warrant and are tapping our land lines and tracking our cell phones. Look, the feds are involved. Several million bucks is a lot of money, yeah, but with all the financial crime out there it's kinda small potatoes. And Moule's murder is a state offense, not a federal one. I suspect there's something bigger here we don't know about."

"What?"

"The person that you met and knew as Moule is a blank

slate. If what they just told us is correct, he was something else before he straightened up in his mid-twenties, got an education and went into currency trading. So who or what was he before? We don't know what's really going on—Labonsky and Hasty just fed us a selected version of the facts. When you think about it, it's pretty obvious that this was not some ordinary heist gone bad, or something like that. The fact that Moule apparently knew one or both of his killers, the transfer of his millions offshore one day before his murder, the FBI's involvement..."

We both sat in silence for a long moment. "So where do we go from here?" I asked.

Holloway didn't answer immediately, evidently still deep in thought. Then, "Look, I know that no matter where this investigation goes, you and I will be okay. Regardless of whatever suspicions those guys might have, our absolute defense is the truth." He hesitated once again, then continued, "If they're trying to frighten one or the other of us, to make us believe they have something incriminating but not strong enough to make an arrest, hoping to push us into making some stupid move, it's not going to work. It's a game, but a game both sides can play. Let's come up with a strategy. Until we clear their suspicions, this whole matter is going to follow us around and hang over our heads like a dark cloud."

"Ideas?"

"Let's both sleep on it overnight and talk about it in the morning. I want to let the whole damned thing percolate through my brain for a while," Holloway replied. "You think about it, too. We'll come up with something." With a promise to call in the morning, I dropped him off at his office.

I called Jessica to be sure all was well at the gallery and told her I'd be in my apartment in the carriage house if she needed me for anything. The carriage house was my refuge, my

61

hideaway, and for the past few years, my home. I had inherited my grandmother's house on her death shortly before my release from prison. One of the conditions of my freedom was that I have gainful employment. Following my grandfather's death years earlier, my grandmother converted the ground floor of their Liberty Street home, a multilevel jewel of Victorian architecture, into an art gallery. Over the years it had become a well-established business and thus an ideal way for me to transition from prison back into the real world. As events would later sort out, I had been told that if I applied to have my disbarment lifted, I would likely be reinstated and could resume the practice of law. But it was too late. I had lost my love for and fascination with the law. The legal system had chewed me up and spit me out, in many ways a broken spirit with no will to fight. At that point in my life I simply wanted to survive. The elegant old house with its ornate furnishings was too much. I moved into the small apartment above the carriage house on the back alley behind the main house and gallery, promising myself that one day, once my life had recovered some semblance of normalcy, I would move into the larger and more ornately furnished rooms facing Liberty Street. As yet, that day had not arrived.

I parked my car in the alley, climbed the steps to the apartment, and sat down in a comfortable chair to think. A number of weeks had passed since Moule's murder, and if what the investigators told us earlier that morning was true, their inquiry had raised more questions than answers. Were we really suspected of some involvement, as Holloway suggested, or was he being paranoid? Any surveillance warrants would be shielded, of course, but even if our phones were being tracked and our calls recorded, neither of us had anything to hide. Still, the possibility bothered me. And then another thought occurred.

What if whoever killed Moule was looking for something but didn't find it? He had moved his monetary assets offshore less than twenty-four hours before his murder. That had to be a last-minute decision and certainly a desperate move, but why? Just the day before he was making plans to meet with me about forming a long-term investment relationship. It just didn't make sense. The police had to know more than they were willing to admit to us. We needed a better feel for where the investigation was headed and how they thought I fit into the picture. After twenty minutes or so of tossing options back and forth in my mind, I decided that we should be aggressively cooperative with the investigation. I could say that I thought I was being helpful by turning over Holloway's report into Moule's background, but now I realized that the detectives must be frustrated, otherwise they wouldn't have asked to meet with me again. And since it appeared that they might suspect my attorney, Phil Holloway, we would both like to be of assistance in any way we could. I didn't want to tackle this alone.

Feeling somewhat better about things, I poured myself a glass of iced tea and headed across the courtyard that separated the carriage house from the rear entrance of the gallery. Jessica was just finishing up a sale with a customer. She smiled and I headed for my office. Ten minutes later she stuck her head in the door and said, "You've been missing the fun. I've sold three paintings thus far today, plus that set of Julius Bien prints of flowers that we've had out for the last several months."

"That's great," I said, smiling back at her. "Anything else going on?"

"Not really. A few phone calls, but nothing I couldn't handle." She turned to see another customer coming in the front door. "Gotta go." She started toward the gallery, then, remembering something, turned back and said, "Oh, I forgot. The

63

cable guy was here. He was working on something out back near the alley. He didn't need to get inside, but wanted me to know what he was up to."

"What cable guy?"

"I don't know. I presumed you called him. I don't watch TV when I'm here, so I didn't know you were having problems." She smiled again and disappeared into the gallery.

There was a problem. I had cancelled the cable subscription six months earlier, preferring the digital superiority and broader access offered by internet video. Hattie paid all the bills. Jessica had no reason to know that I'd made the switch. As soon as she was free I asked her, "What exactly did this guy look like? And what did he say he was doing?"

She seemed alarmed that I would ask. "I don't know, really. He was dressed like a repairman, I guess. Maybe in his late thirties, kinda dark, longish hair. He came in the front door and said he was with the cable company and needed to work on some things in the back, near the alley and the carriage house. He didn't say exactly, and I probably wouldn't know what he was talking about anyway." She paused, frowning. "Is something wrong?"

"I'm not sure. I cancelled our cable subscription a few months ago. Everything's on the internet now. I don't know what he would be working on," I said.

"Oh, dear. I hope I haven't made a mistake. But you set the alarm on your place in the carriage house, don't you? There was no alarm siren or anything."

She was right, but I was still suspicious. The back gate to the courtyard was usually unlocked during the day. The stairs to my apartment above the carriage house led down to the courtyard, but if any door or window of the apartment were disturbed, the alarm would have sounded. "I'm probably overreacting. I'm sure it's nothing, but I'll check out back anyway to be sure everything is secure."

I walked out into the courtyard from the rear entrance to the gallery. The gate to the alley was closed. Except for a random assortment of garbage cans and a small car parked behind someone's house down the block, the alleyway was empty. Looking up, I could see telephone lines and what I assumed were those belonging to the cable company attached to the gable of the carriage house on the second floor above the old garage. Canceling one's cable subscription didn't necessarily mean detaching the wires from the structure. Nothing appeared amiss.

Back in the courtyard, I climbed the steps to my apartment and the small porch in front of my tightly locked door. Entering with my key, I punched the code into the keypad, which beeped to indicate the alarm had been disabled. I checked the windows. All were securely shut and locked. Nothing had been disturbed. I stepped back out on the porch and surveyed the courtyard below. It appeared just the same as it had every day I'd lived there. My porch spanned the entire width of the rear of the building, some twenty-five feet in all, and was sheltered by an enclosed gable supported by exposed rafters. A single battered chair that I had never sat in was next to my front door. Like the rest of the porch floor, it was covered with a thin layer of yellow pollen, the scourge of Southern allergy sufferers. I then noticed a pattern of fresh footprints highlighted by disturbance of the pollen leading from the steps toward the far corner of the porch and back. They appeared to have been made by a larger treaded shoe, consistent with a workman's boot. Now curious, I followed them to the corner and peered up into the shadowed dimness. At first I saw nothing. Then, as my eyes adjusted to the relative darkness, I could just see the edge of a small dark object. I backed away a few feet and peered at it from a different angle. I wasn't sure what it was, but I knew it was not supposed to be there.

Grabbing the chair next to the door, I carefully climbed onto the seat, bringing me within two feet of the lower edge of the rafter, but still not far enough to get a good view of whatever was hidden in the darkness. Gingerly, I reached up blindly to where I thought the object was situated. It appeared to be flat, less than an inch across, about two inches deep, and half an inch or so thick. When I tried to remove it, I realized that it was attached by a wire to something behind it. Reaching further in, I encountered a much larger and heavier object about the size of a cigarette pack. I carefully lifted both of them out, still attached to one another by a short wire. Stepping down from the chair, I turned the objects over in my hand. At first I was confused, but then I realized what I was holding. The larger object was a rechargeable lithium power pack labeled 30,000 mAh. The short wire was a power cord with USB-C connectors on either end. The small, flat object appeared to be a digital camera. Someone had been watching me.

CHAPTER 12

Half an hour later I was back in Holloway's office. The micro camera and its power supply lay between us on the conference room table. After listening quietly as I explained the events leading to its discovery, Holloway shook his head and said, "Damn! If Labonsky and the others are going to stoop this low, I think it's time we started making waves. I could see them bugging our phones, but when you stick a hidden camera on someone's front porch, that's just too much. I mean, they would have to have had specific permission from the judge for something that invasive… What the hell would they be looking for?" He took a deep breath and stared out the window for a moment before continuing. "Okay. Let's do this. We can get all lawyerly and file a bunch of motions asking for discovery and an injunction and whatever, but they'll oppose that and tie things up for weeks, if not longer. Grab the camera and battery. We're heading back downtown. I'll have my secretary call and tell Labonsky to meet us there."

Twenty minutes later we were back in the same conference room where we'd met earlier in the day, waiting for Labonsky to make it back to police headquarters. His assistant, unusually solicitous, offered us coffee or bottled water. We both refused, our demeanor being one of righteous indignation. We had agreed in advance to do a bit of role-playing: me as the aggrieved but innocent party, and Holloway as my bulldog lawyer threatening to publicly expose the totalitarian techniques used by the Savannah police to hassle and intimidate law-abiding citizens. Labonsky arrived a few minutes later, obviously annoyed. "What can I do for you gentlemen? The dispatcher said you sounded upset."

Holloway began, "Throughout the entire time you've been working on this case, Detective, my client has tried to be helpful and supportive of your investigation. He spoke freely with you, answered your questions, and passed on confidential financial and personal information that Mr. Moule had shared with him. Earlier today at your request, we sat in this same conference room while you supposedly gave us an update on your investigation of Moule's murder. Near the end of our conversation, in an off-handed way, you implied that one or the other of us might have been the taller of the two figures captured on video on the morning of Moule's death."

Holloway glanced toward me. I frowned and nodded in agreement as he continued. "In our discussion after leaving this office, it seemed obvious to us that you might indeed be considering one or both of us as possible accessories to this crime, though for what motive or reason I cannot understand. We even discussed the possibility that you'd obtained warrants to track our phone calls and whereabouts electronically despite, I might add, zero evidence to support such an egregious violation of our Fourth Amendment rights." Holloway paused again, as if to allow his words to sink in. "But all that pales in comparison to what appears to be your department's latest scheme. It now appears clear that you invited my client—and me—here so you could attempt to surreptitiously plant this at his residence to monitor his activities and his visitors. You should be ashamed of yourself, Detective." With that, Holloway opened his briefcase and laid the miniature camera and battery apparatus on the table in front of Labonsky.

The detective looked at once both puzzled and distressed. Without speaking, he picked up the device and examined it, turning it over several times in his hands. We watched, waiting for his reply. After a moment he looked up and said, "I have no idea what you are talking about. And I have no idea what this thing here is," pointing at the camera and battery on the table in front of him. He waited for our response.

"It's a camera, Detective. A camera planted at the entrance of Mr. O'Toole's residence presumably for monitoring his activities. And by denying that you know what it is, I presume you're also denying that getting us down here to police headquarters this morning was not in fact a way of getting Mr. O'Toole away from home so one of your men could plant this 'thing,' as you call it. Is that correct?"

"That's correct, Mr. Holloway. Those allegations are ridiculous." Labonsky now seemed genuinely concerned. "To answer your question, yes, we briefly discussed the possibility that either one or both of you might have some involvement in this case, not directly in Moule's killing, maybe as accessories after the fact, hoping to get your hands on some of his assets. But honestly, that didn't make any sense when you think about it, and we dismissed the idea early in the investigation. If we've put any pressure on you, it's to get your full cooperation—to tell us any little piece of the story that you might be holding back."

Labonsky picked up the camera and its battery, once again turning them over several times as if he were looking for some clue he had missed. No one spoke. A siren wailed somewhere in the distance; the deep throaty moan of a ship's horn replied from the direction of the river. He raised his gaze, looking first at me, then at Holloway. "Let me say something that I will ask you to keep confidential. This case, this murder, may be connected to something bigger. We know that Moule's killers are out there somewhere. We have our ideas, but we still don't know exactly why he was killed." Labonsky paused again, assembling his words. "It may be that if we thought you, John,

69

were involved, there are others that might think the same thing. We have no idea who killed Moule, or why, and without an answer to either or both of those questions, we're stymied. If you are willing to work with us on this, maybe I can tell you more. But I've told you too much already. I'll need to get clearance before we discuss this any further."

I looked at Holloway. He looked back at me with an unspoken "it's your call" expression. Turning to Labonsky, I said, "Can you give us a few minutes to talk about this?" Labonsky nodded and left the room, shutting the door behind him.

"What do you think?" I asked.

"Sort of damned if we do and damned if we don't. I don't want to give you my opinion until you tell me how you feel about this situation," Holloway said.

"Okay. First, as hard as it is for me to like Labonsky, I believe we can trust him. Assume for the moment that he's being truthful. In that case, there's too much at stake here for the department to try to pull a stupid move like setting up a hidden surveillance camera outside my apartment. Second, he mentioned 'something bigger,' and they've already called in the FBI—or maybe the FBI heard about the case and stuck their head in. Either way, this may involve things beyond Savannah. We don't know what that means or implies. And thirdly, if the Savannah police didn't plant the camera, someone else did. We know absolutely nothing about who that 'someone' is, why he wants to watch me, what he—or maybe they—ultimately want. You get the picture?"

Holloway nodded.

"So, I say we cooperate. It gives us some degree of protection, not only from whomever appears to have taken an interest in me, but also in the fact that by aligning ourselves with law enforcement we might have access to information and potential threats that we wouldn't otherwise know about," I said.

"I won't argue with your logic," Holloway began, "but as someone who's spent most of his career doing criminal defense work, getting in bed with the cops seems almost, well…dirty. Maybe I've seen too much, but these guys can and will turn on 'cooperating witnesses' like a pack of pit bulls after a prowler."

"We can always back out," I said, "but right now it's a risk I'm willing to take."

Holloway looked down at the table for a moment, then said, "Okay, let's do it."

I opened the conference room door and motioned to Labonsky, who was standing down the hall talking to two other men in suits. He came in and resumed his place at the table. "Well?" he said.

I spoke first this time. "We'll work with you, but we want to make some things clear at the outset. I realize we're civilians and can't be—and don't want to be—part of the investigation, but we want to know what's going on, especially if it involves one or the other of us. If someone is trying to spy on me, I may need protection, or at the very least some good advice about situations that might arise. I don't want to speak for Phil," I said, referring to Holloway, "but the uncertainty of the situation is what bothers *me* the most. If I'm not your target, then who's interested enough to plant a camera at my doorway? There are details, I know, but that will do for a start."

Labonsky looked at Holloway. "And you, Counselor?"

"I agree basically with John, though my level of involvement has to be less because of what I do. Bottom line, though, you have my support."

Labonsky nodded. "Okay, I'll pass this on. Now, I would like you to do something for me—for the investigation. I would like to take this camera or whatever it is and have our IT guys look at it. They can tell a lot more about it than any of us can."

"Okay," I said, quietly relieved that he had asked, "but on the condition that you share the full report with me."

"Done," Labonsky said, then stood up and shook both of our hands.

CHAPTER 13

By midday the following day I had not heard from Labonsky. Holloway called shortly after three o'clock sounding both annoyed and concerned. "This guy, Hasty, the FBI agent who met with us the other day"—he paused to the sound of papers rustling—"I've been on the phone for the last hour and a half, trying to get some background on him, like which division of the Criminal Investigative Division he works for and maybe what case or cases he's assigned to at the moment. It's the sort of information you've got to pry out of your contacts—the Bureau likes to play those things close to the vest." He paused again, taking a deep breath before continuing. "Anyway, here's what I've found out. Hasty's from Atlanta. He's divorced and has a reputation as a loner. He was a senior investigator for the CID, but for most of the past year he's been on loan to DHS, the Department of Homeland Security. What exactly he's doing there is kind of a mystery—at least to the fellows I talked with. The rumor is that he's the Bureau's liaison man on some sort of hush-hush investigation regarding national security, or something like that. The impression from a couple of my contacts is that he's involved in something big. How that intersects with the Moule thing is anybody's guess."

"That's scary," I said. "Maybe Labonsky will fill us in on what's going on."

"Yeah, but in the meantime…" Holloway didn't finish the sentence, but his message was clear. I needed to be very cautious. I knew that.

A sense of uneasiness seemed to have taken over my days. I went about my usual activities, dealing with routine business, occasionally talking to would-be buyers in the gallery, but all the while with the vague feeling that something was wrong. Unfamiliar people—even average customers—seemed to make me uncomfortable, perhaps a little paranoid. Jessica noticed the change and asked if I was all right. "Yeah," I said. "Just a lot on my mind."

"It's not about the cable guy, I hope. I worried all last night about that."

"No, not at all," I lied. "Just routine stuff. You know how it is."

"Sure," she said, her disbelief hiding behind a forced smile.

Labonsky called my cell shortly before the gallery closed that afternoon. "Can you and your attorney meet with me tomorrow? I've gotten permission to fill you in on what's going on, at least in a limited way. And the tech guys have gone over the camera you found at your place. We can talk about that, too." Holloway had informed me earlier that he would be out of town for a few days trying a case in federal court in Valdosta. I told the detective I could meet with him sometime during the afternoon. "Let's, ah…let's meet somewhere less public," Labonsky said. "Do you know the Sandfly Lounge on Fairmont, off Abercorn just beyond the mall? The owner there's a friend of mine." I said I didn't, but could find it. We agreed to meet at two. "The place doesn't open until four," he said. "We'll have some privacy."

The Sandfly Lounge was one of those places that you had to know, not somewhere you'd pop in for a casual drink after work. Located five or so miles south of Savannah's Historic District and adjacent to a military air base, it was tucked away on a side street behind a budget hotel, which itself was half hidden by a low-end strip mall populated by an assortment of equally low-end businesses including an insurance agency, a small loan outlet, and a purveyor of "guns and weaponry."

Except for two cars parked near the motel, the lounge's parking lot was empty when I arrived shortly before two. I pulled into an empty slot in front of the main door and waited. From what I could see, the interior was dark. Five minutes passed, then the front door of the lounge opened just wide enough to see Labonsky beckoning me in.

The Sandfly reeked of beer and cigarettes. To the left of the entry a small dining room's stained carpet was home to half a dozen odd-sized tables and an equal number of booths sprouting out of the windowless walls. To the right, a much larger space surrounded a long U-shaped bar that jutted out into another windowless room with an assortment of high-top tables and stools scattered about. On the far end, a small dance floor was laid in front of a raised platform or stage, the latter evidently serving as the perch for a DJ or small band when the bar was open. Several oversized speakers mounted on stands loomed over either side. Spotlights, now dark but pointed at the stage, could be seen emerging from the dimness of the ceiling above. I followed Labonsky through a set of swinging doors, then through a small kitchen to a private office in the rear of the building. He waved me to a small sofa while he took a seat in a chair facing me. Instead of his usual suit, he was wearing blue jeans and a nondescript sport shirt. "Sorry about the cloak-and-dagger stuff, but I'm trying to keep a low profile," Labonsky said.

"Why?" I asked.

"I'll try to answer that shortly. You didn't sense that you were being tailed, did you? I waited a few minutes before letting you in to see if any cars followed you down the street."

"No, but you didn't warn me to be on the lookout for someone." Now Labonsky was being paranoid, I thought.

"I probably should have, but I only found that out after

we talked yesterday." I didn't reply. For the first time since I'd met him, Labonsky looked uncomfortable, ill at ease about what he had to say. He began, "First, I need to apologize to you for asking you to meet me here like this. Normally, what I should do—what any good police officer should do—is play things by the book, and if I handled it that way, we wouldn't be meeting at all. As much as I hate to admit it, you got pretty well screwed on the Deign case. I played a part in that, although I thought—we all thought—we were doing the right thing at the time. So, I owe you one. I checked with the guys that are in charge of the Moule investigation and they were not at all happy about me filling you in on too many details—I don't think they believe you can be trusted. On the other hand, I think you can, so I'm sticking my neck out to tell you what I'm about to say.

"We haven't really figured out yet who Moule was before he became Moule. We think, however, he might have been involved in some conspiratorial things—domestic terrorism is the word the FBI guys like to use. We've run his fingerprints and DNA against every database available and we've come up with nothing. That's not too surprising; there are a lot of bad guys who keep a very low profile and are often never caught. The thing about Moule, though, is that he went straight. Like a snake, he shed his old skin and grew a new one in the form of a good education, a new career, and a whole new life. And he was successful at it—wildly successful if you measure that by how much money he seems to have made in just a few years. We're theorizing that some of his old friends who knew his secrets looked at him and thought he could do them a lot of good with such things as money laundering or funding for some criminal activity they had in mind. Cryptocurrencies are the ideal vehicle for that. They're totally unregulated, and while they're not as secret or secure as some people would have you believe, there are plenty of opportunities to avoid the prying eyes of governments, the tax people, law enforcement and the like. You with me thus far?"

"I think so," I said.

"Okay. We've run all kinds of possible scenarios, but this is the one we keep coming back to. Moule had gotten rich. There's no doubt about that. He had also forgotten his old friends and the life he lived before he became Moule. I think he was perfectly serious when he approached you about investing in art. He figured art would hold its value over the long run and would be a safe way to divert some of the digital money he'd made into a different class of assets. You said he made some statements about things not being 'real.' You need to know that there are some investigators who have other theories, but that's mine. Anyway, we all seem to agree that something major happened between the last time Moule talked with you and when he was murdered two days later. Apparently on very short notice, he transferred the majority of his assets offshore where only he would have access. We theorize that shortly after he arranged to meet you, someone contacted him with demands and the threat to expose his true identity—it's speculation of course, but it's possible he was being blackmailed." Labonsky stopped, waiting for my response.

I didn't know what to say. "That's hard to believe—"

"Of course," he interrupted. "You wouldn't think some guy walking into your art gallery to buy a painting is a multimillionaire currency trader hiding his secret past life. But that's the way the world works. If someone told you on September 10, 2001, that the following morning a group of Middle Eastern terrorists were going to fly two passenger planes into the World Trade Center in New York, killing nearly three thousand people and starting a war that would kill thousands more, would you have believed it?" We stared at each other in silence for a brief moment, then, "You've got to assume the worst, John, and pray for the best."

"Okay. What do your guys think is going on?" I asked. "What sort of conspiracy or criminal enterprise or however you want to describe it? And how do I come into the picture?"

"The one short answer to both of your questions is that we don't know. About criminal things, there are a wide range of opinions among the investigators. The feds are thinking one thing and our local guys another, but both believe that whoever killed Moule didn't get what they were looking for—access to his money. What they might use it for is still a matter of speculation. And where do you come in? You seem to be the one significant living connection to Moule and his missing millions. I'm assuming he didn't give you any secret passwords or the like before he was offed, but whoever killed him doesn't know that. And we don't know what Moule might have told them." Labonsky studied my reaction then continued, "So they may turn their attention to you. Or already have, assuming the spy camera was planted by someone connected to the murder. And I suspect they may be looking for other ways to see what you might be up to, I just don't know…"

Labonsky's words hit me like a kick in the gut. I swallowed hard and tried to keep my composure. "Tell me about the camera," I said, changing the subject somewhat.

"Yeah, the camera. Again, I had our IT guys go over it. If we had known then what we do now, it might have been helpful to dust it for fingerprints, but at least three of us had handled it by the time I took it to them. The device is simply a small Chinese-made spy camera. You can buy them online or in any number of stores that sell security hardware. The unique thing about this one—or so I was told—is that it's programmable and has Wi-Fi capability. It was set to record short video bursts of thirty seconds when it senses motion. These things can eat power, so the lithium battery was there to provide plenty—probably a couple of weeks at least, they tell me. There were two interesting things. First, the Wi-Fi was programmed to cut on only for about two hours a day between 8:00 and 10:00 a.m. It has sufficient strength for someone walking by your house to pick up the signal and download anything recorded since the previous download. And of course it had a tiny memory card, a 512 gigabyte micro SD, that could probably store weeks of short videos in case someone was unable to download the contents. The device was programmed to reformat the card after each download, erasing the contents and freeing up space if needed. The SD card didn't have anything useful on it, just videos of you when you discovered it. The tech nerds were impressed. They said it had to have been set up by someone who knew what he was doing."

"Or what *she* was doing," I said.

"True. All things are possible in this kind of situation," Labonsky replied.

CHAPTER 14

We talked for another half hour, but Labonsky had delivered the essence of his message. I asked, multiple times and in multiple ways, what I should be doing. Other than the statement "You now know the situation" and the advice to "Be cautious and careful," there was little more he could say or do. "You have my number. I'll be here if you need me," was the only practical assurance he could offer. Our meeting ended when the lounge's employees began to show up for work around three o'clock. I drove back to the gallery in a daze, feeling nothing, my fear and anger replaced by a dull numbness that would allow me to function as long as I did not consider the many negative possibilities the immediate future might hold.

To my surprise and relief, nothing happened. The remainder of the week passed quietly, as did the following weekend. The gallery was doing quite well financially; that brought a bit of joy into my otherwise gloomy existence. Jenna called, several times in fact, but I made excuses about work, fictitious but plausible reasons why we couldn't get together. I didn't want her to see me in my current mood, something she could do nothing to improve and more importantly something I did not want to drag her into. Jessica and Hattie both asked repeatedly if I was all right. Again, I cited vague reasons, labeling them "personal" in an effort to end the inquiry.

As always seems to happen, just when I was beginning to feel some sense of relief, or normalcy, or however you might describe it, events took another strange turn. That was heralded by call from Labonsky on a Tuesday morning just as I was finishing my coffee while sitting in my office at the gallery returning emails. "I just got the word," Labonsky said, obviously excited. "We may have a break in the Moule case. A major one. I thought you'd want to know."

"That's great," I said. "Tell me about it—if you can."

"Well, I just heard the story, second or third hand of course, so I'll need to confirm things and get the facts and details straight, but here's the deal. You remember I told you that we'd submitted Moule's DNA and fingerprints to several national databases, hoping to find a match, or a relative, or really anything that might give us a place to start working toward finding his true identity?" I said I did. "The major national collection of law enforcement DNA data is CODIS—that's short for Combined DNA Index System. It's maintained by the FBI, and all offenders who go through the federal criminal justice system and most of those in the state systems have their DNA profile added to it. So, for example, if there's a rape committed in San Francisco by an unknown perp, it might be possible to make his identity if he had been in prison, even if it was five years earlier and he was clean across the country in, say, New York. So here's what happened—or is happening— I'm not sure. I got this from Hasty this morning.

"With DNA profiles of criminals now available through an easy-to-use system like CODIS, a lot of jurisdictions are going back and looking at their cold cases—you know, the ones that were never solved, especially rapes and murders and child molestation cases where samples were collected before DNA analysis was routine like it is today. We sent Moule's DNA to CODIS not too long after we started investigating his murder. It took a while, but we eventually got word back that no matches were found. We figured that was a dead end. About a month ago, the cold case unit from the Albuquerque Police Department was taking a fresh look at the rape and murder of a woman that happened back in the 1990s. I didn't get a lot of details, but she apparently worked in one of the nightclubs out there and didn't have any close family so far as anyone knew. After she didn't show up for work for a couple of days, her employer called the cops for a welfare check. They found her apartment ransacked, and later the same day her body was discovered by a hiker in the mountains just outside of town. An autopsy showed she'd been assaulted and raped. A specimen of her vaginal washings was collected and kept with other evidence, but again this was before the days of routine DNA testing…" Labonsky speech was rapid and pressured. He stopped to catch his breath. "Are you still with me?" he asked.

"I am."

"Okay, well…it turns out that she had a partial DNA match with Moule. Again, I don't have the details, but she appears to have been a relative—maybe a sister. I think the key thing here is putting the dates together, like when the victim was killed and when the person that became Moule first applied for his social security number and so on."

"But how…," I began, then stopped, waiting for Labonsky to continue.

"There's obviously more to all this, and a lot of work to be done to connect the dots, but I feel that for the first time since we saw you that day at Moule's house we're making some real progress," Labonsky said. He had done the talking while I simply listened. Although he had called me to give an update on the case, it was almost as if he were talking to himself and to the rest of the world, announcing a breakthrough in what seemed like a hopeless quest for an answer, the proverbial light at the end of the tunnel. He was at once excited, elated, hopeful, and expectant of a positive outcome, allowing him to move on to the next case. To some degree, I felt the same emotions, yet with reservations. From my perspective, one unsolved murder—that of Moule—had been linked to another unsolved murder that occurred decades earlier. Did this new revelation mean progress toward solving one or the other or both, or did it just complicate an already complicated case? I wasn't sure, but I thought it best to keep my opinions to myself at this point.

In the back of my mind I wondered why Labonsky had called me with the preliminary news on the breakthrough in the case. More logically, he would have waited until he had more information, a better understanding of what a "partial DNA match" might mean. In the same vein, it might seem strange that he had chosen to meet with me one on one at the Sandfly Lounge, a location far from police headquarters and—I had to assume—from the eyes and knowledge of his fellow cops. Labonsky's words earlier about my getting "pretty well screwed" on the Deign case and that he "owed me one" because of what followed meant just that. Two things came into focus. He believed me and was trying to both protect me and look out for my interests in the Moule murder affair. Perhaps I had become his sounding board, knowing that I would not hesitate to give him feedback on his theories and opinions if I thought it appropriate. He realized now that he should have believed I was telling the truth in the Deign matter.

All I could do now was wait. It appeared that nothing had come of the hidden camera incident, at least nothing I was aware of. Perhaps it was totally unrelated to Moule's murder. Savannah has a plentiful share of other criminals, including those who might want to monitor my apartment or business for a possible break-in. I had done all that I could, and it was time I tried to purge the lingering uncertainty from my mind.

The gallery continued to do a brisk business. On Friday of the same week, Jessica asked me if I'd help her with a client, a lady who had just moved to Savannah and was looking for a larger piece of art to hang in her new apartment. She led me to a striking brunette surveying a larger abstract work in bright acrylics painted by a local artist. "Sarah, I'd like you to meet John O'Toole, the gallery's owner. He can answer your questions and tell you pretty much anything else you need to know." Jessica grinned, half snickering at her attempt to be witty.

Sarah turned, smiled, and held out her hand. "John, it's so good to meet you. Jessica says you know everything there is to know about art, so maybe you can help me decide on a piece to hang over my fireplace." I studied her eyes as she spoke. Sarah was, in a word, beautiful. Not in the sense of glamour or fashion, but instead a confident, physically attractive woman in her early to mid-thirties who exuded an air of poise and self-assurance.

"I'll be happy to try," I said, smiling back. "What sort of questions did you have?"

"Well, first let me say that I've just moved to town. I've been living in Atlanta for the last decade and—I hate to say it—just finished up what's been a very difficult divorce. I needed a change. I've always liked Savannah, so here I am. I've taken a six-month lease on a furnished apartment downtown, on Bay Street across from Factors Walk. If I like it, I'll stay longer. If not, or if I find a place better suited, I'll move there. Anyway, I sort of want to personalize the place as long as I'm there, and I thought a good work of art would be a good way to start."

"We're happy to be of assistance," I said. "I see you were looking at this piece by Jethro Hardwick. He's a local artist with a national reputation. A graduate of SCAD—the Savannah College of Art and Design—and lives out toward Tybee—

the beach, you know."

"Yes, I went exploring out that way when I was looking for a place to stay. But I prefer this part of town, the Historic District, in fact, my place is not that far from here.

About half a mile, I'd guess. Just far enough for a pleasant walk. Let me tell you a little about Hardwick and his art..." For the next ten minutes we talked. I showed Sarah a couple of other Hardwick canvases we had on display. She asked intelligent, insightful questions and listened carefully as I answered, watching me closely as I spoke.

After hearing my thoughts and recommendations, Sarah said, "I think I'd like to buy the one I was looking at when Jessica first introduced us. But would it be possible to sort of see it in place before I say for sure? You never really know how a painting will look in a room until you actually see it on the wall. Since I want to hang it over the fireplace, we could just prop it on the mantel. If that works, I'll give you a check."

I told her that sounded good to me. The piece was only $700, relatively inexpensive compared to most works of that size in the gallery. I told her I could deliver it.

"I've got some errands to run before the end of the day," Sarah said. "Would it be asking too much to get you to bring it over after work, say about 6:30 or 7:00? There'll still be plenty of daylight then."

"Sure," I said. "I think I'll Uber over and walk back, assuming you decide you want this painting."

"I'm almost certain I will. And as long as you're there, maybe you can stay for a drink." Sarah touched my hand. A small chill ran down my back.

CHAPTER 15

Sarah said, "That sounds good," and wrote her address and cell number on a piece of paper that she handed to me, her face beaming. "I'll see you this evening—and if you're running late, don't worry. I'm free all night." There was something suggestive in her voice.

Jessica, who had been standing by quietly listening to the entire conversation with her arms folded over her chest, frowned as Sarah left the gallery. "Well! She's an interesting character."

"How do you mean?" I asked.

"Just in case it wasn't obvious…I guess I should have said 'interested' rather than 'interesting.'" I glanced back at her with a neutral expression. "I know she's a customer, John, and if she buys the Hardwick that's a great sale, but I can't help but think she wants something extra, a throw-in of sorts."

"How do you mean?" I wrinkled my brow as I spoke.

"Well, in case it's not completely, totally, and utterly obvious, she wants you, a least for a quick encounter if not more…" Jessica was frowning now.

"Maybe, yeah, but we're in the business of selling art and she's a buyer. We'll keep it on that level," I said. Jessica made a little sound that resembled a snort and headed back to her desk. I have to admit that I'm not a complete fool. It was obvious that Sarah was coming on to me, and from a strictly male standpoint I found her attractive and appealing. But the last thing I needed at the moment was a relationship—or another relationship, I should say. I had Jenna, with whom I had a history, someone I cared about dearly. Tempting, to be sure, but one of the first rules of any profession is never mixing business with pleasure.

I carefully bundled up the Hardwick painting, covering it so that it wouldn't be damaged in the process of delivering it. It was roughly three feet high and four feet wide, so I needed to be sure that I ordered a larger vehicle for the trip if I was going to Uber over to Sarah's place. I ate a light supper and at 6:45 summoned a ride on my cell phone. It turned out that an Uber XL was cruising the neighborhood; a driver with a black Ford Explorer pulled up in front of the gallery on Liberty Street in less than ten minutes. With the help of the driver, we loaded the painting into the back and headed toward the Bay Street address Sarah had given me.

Sarah's building was in an ideal location, facing the Bay Street park and Factors Walk, and beyond that River Street and the mighty Savannah flowing toward the Atlantic. Several stories in height, it had, like many buildings in the former downtown business district, been converted to apartments or condos. The driver parked on a side street while I removed the painting and carried it to the Bay Street front entry. I pressed the button for Sarah's apartment, which was followed shortly by a click as the inner door unlatched, leading me to a small lobby and a pair of elevators. Her unit was on the fifth floor. She greeted me beaming as the door opened. "I'm really glad you could deliver the painting so quickly. I'm eager to see how it will look."

The apartment had two bedrooms and faced a parking lot between buildings. It was relatively small but neat and well furnished. The fireplace, while having a hearth and mantel, appeared to be more decorative than functional. I balanced the painting on the mantel as Sarah watched from across the room. She walked about peering at it from this angle and that before pronouncing, "I like it." Turning back to me she said, "You've sold it. Thank you so much."

As I watched her move about the room, I could not help being fascinated. There was something almost indefinable in the way she moved, the way she tilted her head when studying the painting, the way she adjusted the window blinds and turned lamps on and off to see how it appeared in varying lights. The word "attractive" popped in my mind, followed almost immediately by a vision of Jessica standing next to me saying "Like a moth to a flame."

"Let's celebrate with a drink," Sarah said. "I make a great piña colada, complete with Bacardi 151 Puerto Rican rum."

"I'd love one, but if you don't mind, make mine without the rum. I try to avoid alcohol." What I really wanted to say was that I didn't need anything to impair my better judgment, and 151-proof rum would no doubt do just that.

"Sure," Sarah said, her voice cheery. "It's still just as tasty." She motioned toward a small couch. "Make yourself comfortable while I whip things up in the kitchen." We talked as she worked—the tiny kitchen was little more than an alcove off the larger central room. She said that she eventually wanted to find a job here in Savannah, but she'd received a large settlement in the divorce and would take her time before deciding what to do. I told her I was divorced also. She asked, pointedly, if I were seeing anyone. Swallowing hard, I said that I was. "Well, I wouldn't have thought otherwise, a handsome man like you," she replied with a giggle.

From the kitchen, the sound of a blender was followed by the tinkle of glassware and Sarah emerging with a tray holding two tall glasses and a small bowl of salted cashews. "Okay, two piña coladas, one full strength for me and one virgin for you. Yours is garnished with a cherry." She passed the glass to me, placed the tray on the coffee table, and sat down within arm's reach on the couch. Raising her glass, she said, "It's good to make a new friend."

Gingerly, I lifted the cherry-garnished glass to my lips. A quick sniff—no alcohol. I took a small sip. Again, no alcohol, and certainly not any 151-proof rum. As she had at our first encounter, Sarah was watching me closely. "No, I didn't spike your drink, though I'll have to admit the idea crossed my mind. You're an attractive man, John."

I took another drink, a longer one this time. "Thank you, Sarah. And you're an attractive woman." There was a moment of awkward silence. I tried to push the subject in another direction. "The painting looks great in this room. It goes perfectly with the decor."

"Yes, it does, but I rented this apartment furnished. I've left most of my stuff—furniture, even clothes—in storage until I decide exactly what I want to do, where I want to live. You live downtown. Would you want to live elsewhere? Maybe Wilmington Island, or even further south down the coast around St. Simons or Sea Island? It's a tough decision."

I reached out and grabbed a few cashews, followed by another swallow of my drink. "I spent much of my childhood here in Savannah. The house—the gallery—belonged to my grandparents. I inherited it when I—" I caught myself just as I was about to say, "got out of prison."

Sarah set her drink on the table and waited for me to finish my sentence. Furrowing her brow, she asked, "When, John? You inherited it when?"

"Just before I moved back here to Savannah." I was suddenly beginning to feel strange. It was as if things around me were slowing down, that my voice sounded like a recording run at half-speed.

"Didn't you mean to say 'when I got out of prison?'" Sarah

said, her voice suddenly cold.

"I…, I…," I began, but my mouth wouldn't form the words. My now half-empty glass slipped out of my grip and rolled away, spilling the milky-yellowish liquid on the carpet. That was the last thing I remembered.

CHAPTER 16

As best I can recall, I was awakened sometime later by a persistent, annoying buzzing. I had a throbbing headache, my mouth was dry, and for a moment I had no idea where I was or how I might have gotten there. I opened my eyes and tried to raise my head off the pillow behind it. The world began to spin, so I closed them and eased back down. After a moment, I tried again, this time glancing about with as little motion of my head as possible. It appeared that I was in a small bedroom. There was a bedside table with a lamp and an alarm clock, which was the source of the buzzing. I blindly groped in its direction until I found it and slammed my fist into it. The buzzing stopped. Sunlight streamed in through a single window whose yellow curtains were held open by silk ropes. With the buzzing ended, I could hear traffic noises and a ship's horn in the distance. Then I remembered: Sarah. The apartment on Bay Street. The piña colada. And did she really ask me about prison, or did I dream that? How could she know? It had to be a dream, I decided. And where was she now? I must have passed out, but did she put me in bed? I looked down at my bare chest and, feeling lower, realized that I still had on my pants. Across the room I could just make out my shirt and undershirt hanging neatly on the back of a chair. My shoes were on its seat. On the bedside table I could see my wallet, keys, and wristwatch. I fumbled for my watch to learn that the time was 9:28 a.m. Someone had put me to bed, but to my horror, I had no recollection of anything at all beyond spilling the remainder of my drink on the carpet. More than thirteen hours were missing.

With the slowest deliberation, I threw back the covers and gradually sat up on the side of the bed. The room spun. I felt nauseous. I closed my eyes and held them shut until the spinning stopped and the urge to vomit passed. The door to the bedroom was open a few inches; I could see a lighted hall just beyond. I realized that I would have to face—and apologize to—Sarah. I'd made a fool of myself, but then I also remembered that I hadn't drunk anything—or had I? The events of the evening before were becoming a mixed-up blur. I needed to find a bathroom. Staggering toward the door, I pulled it open to realize that the bedroom where I'd slept was adjacent to a bathroom whose door was open and lights on. I lurched in, shut the door, and spent the next ten minutes hugging the toilet as I vomited until there was no more to come up.

Feeling marginally better, I stood up, faced the mirror over the sink and surveyed the damage. My eyes were bloodshot, my face puffy. Hoping to find some mouthwash or toothpaste or something, I opened the cabinet behind the mirror. It was empty. I saw a small closet. It contained towels and washcloths, but nothing else. A laundry hamper was bare.

Staggering out into the hall, I called, "Sarah?" There was no answer. The door just in front of me was partially open. I stuck my head in to see the second bedroom, somewhat larger, with a door to a second bathroom open to the side. The bed was neatly made. The double doors of a large closet were standing open; the closet was empty. This bedroom's bath, like the first one, was empty as well. No toothbrush, no dirty towels, nothing. It looked like it had not been used at all.

At this point I began to question my sanity. The night before I had delivered a painting to an apartment in a building on Bay Street where a client said she lived. Something happened. Now I found myself in what appeared to be an uninhabited furnished apartment. I staggered down the short hall to the main room, half expecting to see Sarah perched on the couch, angry at my indiscretion. No one was there. It was the same as the night before. The furniture and the faux fireplace were unchanged, and the painting by Jacob Hardwick still sat on the mantel. A note was propped in front of it. Unsteadily, I walked over, careful not to trip on the coffee table. I noticed that the tray and drink glasses were gone, and it appeared that the mess I had made when I spilled my drink had been cleaned up. Or had that never happened and I just imagined it?

The note, written on plain paper in the same script as Sarah's address and phone number, said, "Sorry, John. I changed my mind about the painting. There are some other things we need to discuss, though. We'll be in touch." It was signed "Sarah."

I was desperately thirsty. I turned toward the kitchen, eager for a cool glass of water or maybe some of the pineapple juice Sarah had used to make the drinks the night before—then it struck me. Perhaps I'd been deliberately drugged. I needed to get a sample of the juice or the coconut cream or even the cherry that garnished my drink for analysis. I needed to know what happened. But the kitchen, like the bedrooms and bathrooms, was pristinely neat and clean. The refrigerator was totally empty, as was the dishwasher. Plates and glasses were neatly arranged in the cabinets. A small bit of water in the bottom of the sink suggested that someone had used it to wash something, but that must have been hours ago.

I leaned against the counter, not knowing what to do. I could call Phil Holloway, but I was embarrassed to try to explain to him how I got myself in this situation, even though I was sure he'd understand. Labonsky could help me, I was sure of that, but he wasn't my attorney or my friend. Bringing him in might involve the police in ways I couldn't predict. I needed to call someone for advice or direction—but where was my phone? As I recalled, it had been in the left back pocket of my pants, but I checked and nothing was there. Now panicking, I rushed back into the smaller bedroom, my eyes darting about for the missing phone before I found it, neatly propped up in one of my shoes on the chair along with my shirt and undershirt. For the first time since I'd woken, a wave of relief seemed to sweep over me. But the phone wouldn't boot up. It had been more than twenty-four hours since I'd charged it. The battery was dead.

Hurriedly, I put on my clothes, stuffed Sarah's note in my shirt pocket, grabbed the painting, and headed down to Bay Street. I hailed the first cab I saw, stowing the canvas in the back seat while I rode in the front with the driver. The cabbie said, "Did you have a bad night, man? You look a little the worse for wear."

"Yeah, women," I said, making a neutral male excuse.

"I know," he said, shaking his head. "Been there and done that. I could tell you stories…"

I thought if I ever figured out what had happened the night before, I'd have one to tell him, but instead nodded and kept my eyes on the street to avoid the waves of nausea that seemed to be returning. We were back at the gallery in a matter of minutes. I had the cabbie drop me off in the rear alley and paid the fare with a generous tip. I noted that the cash and credit in my wallet appeared undisturbed.

I struggled up the stairs to my apartment, lugging the painting. The door was locked and the alarm was on, indicating nothing had been disturbed. Or so it seemed. The first thing I did was put my phone on the charger followed by a cold bottle of water and a long hot shower. As I toweled off, my phone beeped, alerting me to a text message. I picked it up, noting that the battery was charged to fifteen percent, a sufficient level to send and receive texts and make a call or two. I tapped the text message icon and immediately recognized the number as that of Sarah. Now, almost trembling, I touched the screen. Her message was brief and to the point:

> It looks like you made it home. That's good. It appears that you had a great time last night. I'm sure you would want to keep this private, especially from certain people, like Jenna. We searched your place while you were napping but don't worry, we didn't steal or disturb anything. We believe you have something we want. We will be in touch sometime soon. In the meantime, don't worry. We'll be keeping an eye on you.

The text was signed "Sarah."

Accompanying the text was a photograph, apparently taken in the same bed where I had awoken a couple of hours earlier. I was lying on my back, my eyes closed, with the covers pulled up to just above my waist. Cuddled next to me was a dark-haired female, her head on my right shoulder but turned toward me so that her face was not visible. The rest of her body was, however, from the tips of her toes to the nape of her neck. Her right arm was folded over my body, with her hand over my heart. We both appeared to be totally naked. Was it possible that I had sex with Sarah and couldn't remember it? But then who took the photo?

Another wave of nausea swept over me. I rushed toward the bathroom to throw up.

CHAPTER 17

I needed to talk to someone—someone who wouldn't judge and condemn me when I confessed that I had screwed up badly. Jessica and Hattie were out. There was Jenna, but how do you confess to the one person in the world you're closest to that you ended up in bed with a naked woman you'd only met hours before? Excuses—no matter how legitimate—wouldn't work. Would she really believe someone had drugged me? There was Labonsky, but this new development opened a can of worms. He needed to know, but first I needed some cool-headed advice about explaining what happened. The only person from whom I could expect a calm, objective appraisal of the situation, and who could advise me how to proceed, was Phil Holloway. No doubt he would think I was an idiot for getting into such a mess, but the clients of most criminal defense attorneys are textbook examples of bad judgment and appalling stupidity. I dialed Holloway's cell number. After what seemed like an interminable delay, Phil picked up, saying, "Hey, John. What's up?" He sounded rather cheery. I told him I needed his advice. "Sure, but can it wait?" he said. "We're about to go out to dinner."

"Uh, maybe. Where are you?"

"We just left Piraeus, headed to Santorini. We'll arrive there in the morning."

The names sounded familiar. I tried to cut through my mental fog to remember where I'd heard them. "Are you in Florida?" I asked.

Phil burst out in a hearty laugh. "That's great, John." Apparently speaking to someone near him, he said, "He wants to know if we're in Florida." Then back to me, "Not quite. We're in the eastern Mediterranean somewhere between Greece and Turkey. You forgot, it's our twenty-fifth wedding anniversary. We've been planning this cruise for more than a year."

I should have known, or better, I should have remembered. Phil had told me months earlier that he and Carol were taking a two-week vacation to celebrate, but it had completely slipped my mind. "So what's going on?" Phil asked. "I don't mind you calling, of course, but we're seven hours ahead of you over here."

"It's nothing really," I said, trying to sound casual. "Just a few things that can wait until you two get back. So have fun. Drink a glass of champagne for me."

"We will, every night," Phil said. The line clicked as the connection went dead.

That left Labonsky. I called his cell phone. "What do you need, John?" he answered, recognizing my caller ID and sounding just a shade annoyed. "It's Saturday. I've finally managed to get a day off. What can I do for you?"

"I've got a problem," I began. "A big problem…"

I outlined in broad strokes the series of events that started Friday afternoon with my meeting Sarah, and my situation at the moment, late Saturday morning. "Good God, your world sure changed overnight." Labonsky said. "Who is this woman, and who's working with her? I haven't seen it, but I have a feeling that the photo of you wasn't exactly a selfie she set up and took. It sounds like you were drugged—"

"Yeah," I interrupted him, "but my memory is just jumbled up. Like I said, the last thing I remember is spilling my drink, but obviously something happened—a lot of things happened—after that. And I don't understand what she said in the text about 'searching' my place. She used the word 'we.' Do you think someone was with her, and how could they have

97

gotten in? I set the alarm when I left, and it was on when I came home. I just…"

Labonsky butted in. "You're on your cell phone, right?"

"Yeah."

"Okay. Let's end this conversation now. I'll be at your place in twenty minutes. Power your cell off now," he commanded and hung up without a further word.

The alleyway gate was open. Labonsky pulled up in the courtyard below my apartment driving a worn two-decade old Ford pickup. He leaped out, dressed in blue jeans, boots, and a faded sweat-stained tee shirt emblazoned with an Atlanta Braves logo. "Sorry about my appearance. I was trying to get some yardwork done. I want to go over everything—starting with when you met this Sarah person."

"Let's go inside," I said. "It's cooler."

"Yeah, but I'm guessing that if they searched your place they may have bugged it, too. Let's take a ride in my truck. It's a good disguise. And your phone's off, right?" I nodded. "Good. Leave it here."

We headed west and north on Highway 21 toward Rincon and Springfield, riding in silence for the first ten minutes while Labonsky negotiated city traffic. As we crossed I-95, he said, "Tell me again about everything that happened. Try to remember every little detail." Once again, but this time more slowly, I recounted my meeting with Sarah, our conversation at the gallery, my arrival at her apartment, and everything I could recall after she served me the piña colada.

"You said Sarah told you she'd rented the place furnished and had been living there how long?"

"I don't know exactly. She said she had a six-month lease, but we didn't leave the main room with the fireplace," I said. "I didn't use the bathroom or see the inside of either bedroom or…"

"But I take it you had that in mind," Labonsky said. I didn't answer. With that, the conversation stopped. After a few awkward moments, he said, "Sorry. That was uncalled for."

"Well, you may be right, but…," I began.

"Don't try to explain. We've all been there. Let's think about what we're going to do. I keep going back and forth in my mind trying to decide if I should share this with the other fellows working on the Moule thing or not. I mean, we don't really know that there's any connection between the two. Maybe this chick is just out to blackmail you or something. But on the other hand, you're the one thing, the one person that's also connected to Moule." He paused, thinking. "Let me do this. I'll talk with one of the investigators who's a good friend. We'll check on the apartment rental and see what we can come up with on the phone number Sarah used to contact you. I'll personally check your place for bugs and hidden cameras. Do you have another cell phone—like one for the gallery maybe?"

"No. Why?" I asked.

"You've got to worry about someone tracking your location through your phone," Labonsky explained. "There are plenty of spyware programs that can be used for that. If you don't believe me, ask any divorce attorney whose client has tracked their husband or wife. We still don't know what these people want with you—or *from* you. I think you'd better leave your cell phone powered off. Go to Walmart or somewhere like that and get one of those cheap prepaid phones. Forward calls from your cell to the new number and block your outgoing number on the new phone. That's what we routinely do for confidential informants. If you'll let me take your phone to the station, I'll get the CSI guys to check it for spyware and have a

99

look at the photo she texted you. Sometimes cell phone photos have encrypted data that's useful. All this will take at least a day or two. If I can get someone working on it today, I should know something by Monday afternoon or Tuesday at the latest."

With a plan in place, we headed back toward Savannah, stopping briefly at the Walmart Supercenter just south of Rincon to purchase a Nokia flip phone with a hundred prepaid minutes. Back at my apartment, I turned on my old cell phone long enough to forward my calls to the new number, then cut it back off before handing it to Labonsky. "You said you wanted to check my place for bugs?" I asked.

"I do, yeah, but it's late. I need to get my things to do that. Like I said, I hope to hear something back on the apartment and maybe this phone by early next week. I'll come over then and check things."

"In the meantime?" I asked.

"Just take it easy. Assume someone is watching or listening, and don't do anything that you wouldn't want that someone to see or hear." Simple advice for sure, but almost guaranteed to induce paranoia, I thought. On the other hand, my life was generally pretty dull.

It was Tuesday afternoon before Labonsky contacted me. Sunday and Monday brought no news one way or the other. As things worked out, Jessica had taken Saturday off, asking Hattie to work in her place. Fortunately for me, Hattie hadn't noticed my slinking back to my apartment or Labonsky's visit during the day. On Sunday with the gallery closed, I quietly replaced the Hardwick painting on the wall, later commenting to Jessica that Sarah had decided against buying it. "Well, I'm not surprised," she said. "I think she was just interested in getting you over to her place so she could interview you in private." I muttered some nonspecific response, praying silently that she would never learn the truth.

Labonsky called my new cell number, saying he wanted to come over and talk with me about what he'd discovered. "There's a lot," he said. He promised to bring his gear to check my place for bugs and hidden cameras. We sat in his truck in the alleyway, out of range of any digital spies. "Sometimes I think I have one of the most stressful jobs in the world, dealing every day with violence and murder, but this thing is about to get to me. I almost don't know where to start," he admitted.

First, the phone that Sarah had called me from was—like my new Nokia flip phone—a prepaid burner phone from Walmart. His sources—off the record, I was sure—told him the phone had not been used to make a call since Saturday and was apparently powered off, as it didn't register a signal in or near Savannah. The condo that Sarah had allegedly leased for six months was owned by a couple from Raleigh, North Carolina, who had purchased it as a vacation home. The building had a strict no-subleasing or short-term rental policy, but the owners were quietly ignoring the rule and renting the unit via a "vacation rental by owner" site on the web. A man named Jonathan McCurdy called about two weeks prior to Sarah's visit to the gallery and rented the unit for four weeks, paying in advance with a money order that had been purchased at a convenience store in Atlanta. The store had a security camera system, but videos were only available for about a week and then recorded over to save storage space. "The condo owners are now in deep crap with the building's condo owner association," Labonsky commented.

"And the photo...," Labonsky said, choosing his words carefully, "it's..., ah...interesting, to say the very least. Here's a blowup of the image we recovered from your phone." His gaze lingered a moment before he continued. "She—the person you know as Sarah—is quite naked, as you can see. I think every CSI guy on the force 'studied' it, but we had two remarkable and important observations. Look here," he said, pointing at her right arm draped over my chest. "See, just behind the shoulder on her upper back, there's something there." He reached in an envelope and extracted a second blowup focusing on the area. "She has a tattoo. You can only make out about half of it, but it appears to be some sort of unusual geometric figure. I've got one of the force's sketch artists trying to draw what it might look like. We've got more work to do on that. It could be important though." He looked at me for my reaction.

"I don't recognize the shape—maybe the sketch will be helpful," I said. "And what's the second thing?"

"Oh, that could be important, too. One of the guys who works in our local crime lab—he's a trained technician and kind of a ladies' man, if you know what I mean. He pointed out one thing. Look here. What color do you see?" He pointed at the naked figure's pubic hair.

"I don't know. Kinda light colored, blondish maybe," I said. Why would this guy—why would anyone—be interested in the color of someone's pubic hair?

"Right," Labonsky said. "And the hair on Sarah's head?"

"Dark. Brunette."

"Right." Labonsky watched me, waiting for my response.

"Oh, yeah." I realized where this was going. "She's likely a natural blonde."

"Exactly. And if you will recall, one of the two visitors to Moule's house on the day he was killed appeared to be…"

"…a blonde female," I said, finishing his sentence.

CHAPTER 18

"What about my phone?" I asked.

"Oh, yeah. That's something else," Labonsky said. "You have an iPhone, right? Well, we don't normally have the kind of experts who can figure out if a phone's been bugged or fixed to secretly give out the location to someone monitoring it, but one of our guys just got back from training and was up on all the latest tech. He tells me that someone installed a Pegasus spyware program on your phone. Like I told you before, I don't understand a lot of how this is done, but the program was originally created by an Israeli cyber-arms company and is capable of accessing your phone's camera, microphone, and emails, in addition to allowing you to be tracked. It's a pretty powerful program. He was really surprised to find it— mostly government and spy types use it, or so he was told." Labonsky saw the look on my face. "Maybe you better plan on permanently getting rid of that phone and switching to another.

"And you'd asked about how Sarah might have gotten in your apartment, if that actually happened. My guys tell me that she almost certainly put something in your drink. I talked with about five of them and the general feeling was that it was most likely one of two drugs. First, there's chloral hydrate. It's a drug that's been around for way more than a hundred years—back in the day it was used as a sleeping med, but hasn't been in recent decades. It's still available in liquid or powder form and works very quickly. And then there's fentanyl—you recall we found that in Moule's system at autopsy. That's also a rapidly acting drug that can be slipped in a drink and then—assuming you don't OD on it—mostly be out of your system in just a few hours. Whatever it was, though, once you're drugged you could easily tell someone the password to your alarm system and have no recollection of it the following morning. That may be what happened—I don't know."

I sat in stunned silence. I'd heard of chloral hydrate and "slipping someone a Mickey," but never in my wildest dreams did I think I might be on the receiving end. And fentanyl—I'd read somewhere just days earlier that it had become one of the leading causes of death from drug overdoses. I could have died.

Labonsky said, "Let's check your place for bugs. Since Sarah—or someone—installed the Pegasus program on your phone, it would seem less likely that they'd also try to hide spy gear in your apartment." For the next twenty minutes he poked about with a small radiofrequency detector and a separate laser scan, seeking signals from occult microphones or the reflections of laser light from lenses of hidden cameras. I watched with a morbid sense of fascination. After prodding every possible nook and cranny Labonsky announced, "Looks like you're clean."

"Good," I said. "That's the first positive thing I've heard today."

"Okay," Labonsky said. "I've got to get cleaned up and head down to headquarters. I have no idea how all this crap is going to tie in with Moule's murder and the other bigger things that attracted the feds, but every little piece of the puzzle is potentially important. I need to write a report while it's fresh in my mind."

"You're not going to put in the part about Sarah or whatever her name is and"—I hesitated—"the photo?" I had a vision of my name on the front page of the *Morning News* with a headline reading "Former Suspect in Deign Murder Case Involved in Sex Scandal."

"John, wake up," Labonsky said. "Of course I am. It's part

of the case. It's evidence, clues, whatever you want to call it. I'm a homicide cop. We deal with this type of shit—and worse—every day." With that he left, his aging pickup trailing a small cloud of blue smoke.

I sat alone in my apartment, the silence broken only by the humming of the air conditioner, a vital necessity in summertime Savannah. Once upon a time I had a bright future: a family, a successful career, a generous income, and the eventual prospect of a long and peaceful retirement in some secluded mountain community, punctuated by visits from my grandchildren and leisurely vacations to exotic destinations. But it had all fallen apart for causes and reasons I could not have prevented or controlled. Perhaps it was my hubris that brought me down. It was as if I had unknowingly offended some hidden deity who was now wreaking his—or her—vengeance in order to teach me a lesson, to humble me. If that were its goal, it had nearly succeeded. I wasn't sure how much more I could take. It had to stop one way or another. I heated a can of chicken noodle soup for supper and went to bed shortly thereafter.

My cell phone rang at seven the next morning. I didn't recognize the number but answered it anyway. "Mr. O'Toole?" a male voice said. "Jim Hasty here." It took me a few seconds to recall that Hasty was the FBI agent assigned to the Moule investigation. "I apologize for disturbing you this early," Hasty continued, "but I wanted to fill you in on the latest info that we received overnight from Albuquerque. Are you available sometime today?"

"I can be, if it's important." I didn't know if I could stomach any more surprises.

"It is, very much so. It may be the break in the case that we've been looking for. That's why I called you first thing."

"That's good news, I take it?"

"Looks like it. Can you meet me at police headquarters at ten o'clock this morning? I know Rod Labonsky has been keeping you up to speed, but he left on a plane to Atlanta an hour ago with connections to Albuquerque. He asked me to get in touch with you early this morning."

"I'll be there," I said, as unspoken waves of fear, relief, and anticipation swept through my thoughts.

Three hours later I found myself waiting in the now familiar conference room in the headquarters building on the corner of Oglethorpe and Habersham. The heat had not yet overwhelmed the day, so I had walked from the gallery, thinking the exercise might ease my anxieties. Hasty was late, breezing in with an apology and a thick folder stuffed with documents. "Sorry to keep you waiting, Mr. O'Toole...," he began.

"Call me John, please."

"Sure. Well, again I apologize, John. It's just after eight in Albuquerque and I needed to talk to an agent there to get a few things straight before I presented this to you. As you know, normally we would not be sharing this information, but you've become an integral part of the ongoing case and can possibly offer some insights and assistance in figuring out how the moving parts are connected. If you don't mind, let me just start and go through how we got here and what we know—and don't know—and what questions we have. That okay?"

I nodded.

"Then I'll get started. As I think Rod Labonsky told you, the Albuquerque police have a cold case squad and have been following up on unsolved crimes—especially murders and rapes—when they have possible DNA evidence that might help identify a unknown assailant. Several months ago they got around to looking at the case of Penny Lovelace, a thirty-five-year-old white female who was raped and murdered there in the city. Her body was found in the mountains near town in April 1996. According to the autopsy report, she'd been dead for about twenty-four hours. There was some evidence in the case file that the team thought might contain DNA from her killer, so they submitted that to the CODIS database, plus a separate sample to determine the victim's DNA. Well, to make a long story short, her DNA—not that of her presumed killer—was a partial match with a sample of Donald Moule's DNA that the Savannah cops had sent to CODIS. Got it thus far?"

"I'm following," I said.

"Okay, well, I asked the FBI Albuquerque field office to look into this to see if there might be a connection to the Moule case here. And I need to remind you at this point that I am not authorized to discuss with you why the FBI has an interest in these cases, but we do. So, here in this folder are copies of the original investigation reports, the interviews, the autopsy, and so on. Let me summarize these for you.

"Penny Lovelace was not an angel. She apparently first showed up in Albuquerque around 1980 or '81 when she would have been nineteen or twenty years old. She got a social security number in 1981 and, based on her employment history, worked as a waitress in a series of nightclubs for most of her life. The investigators at the time of her death determined that in fact she started off as a stripper and later became an escort, or to put it more accurately, a hooker. She had three arrests for prostitution over several years in her late twenties and early thirties. Apparently her career, if you can call it that, went downhill as she aged. There was also a question of drug use, but that was not found to have contributed to her death— she was strangled, by the way. At the time of her murder, police were unable to establish that she had any living relatives—her body was eventually buried in a pauper's grave. They couldn't determine where she lived before she appeared in Albuquerque. It was assumed that she was a runaway and for whatever reason had cut all ties with her family."

"A sad tale, for sure," I said, "but tell me more about the DNA match."

"I'm getting to that, but the background is important," Hasty said. "Lovelace lived life on the edge." He tapped on the folder of documents. "In these interview reports recorded by investigators at the time, it's said that she moved frequently, was often in trouble financially, those sort of things. When the cold case squad first got the report back on the partial match between Lovelace's and Moule's DNA profiles, it was assumed that they were siblings, though Moule would have been about fifteen years younger. With the preliminary match, the lab took a deeper dive into the analysis. Apparently Lovelace and Moule were not siblings. She appears to have been his mother."

CHAPTER 19

It's strange, but the first thought that flew through my mind was that it never occurred to me that Moule might have a mother. Of course he did, as we all do, but the very idea begged the question of what sort of family, what sort of home environment, what sort of childhood influences would produce a man like Moule? If Penny Lovelace was in fact the mother of Donald Moule, did she attempt to raise him while living on the margins of society? Or had she, in abandoning whatever family or past she might be running from, abandoned him as well? If so, who became his adopted family? It would appear that Lovelace would have been only fifteen when Moule was born. Surely it would not have been a planned pregnancy. Then I remembered, when we first met, Moule said his family was from Nova Scotia in Canada. I told Hasty. "Moule told me his family came from Nova Scotia."

Hasty's eyes widened. "You're kidding?"

"No. It was something he mentioned casually the first time we met. That's all I remember about the conversation. I didn't mention it before because it didn't seem important."

"That's a start," Hasty said, evidently excited. "I suspect the entire province has fewer people than many cities in the US—and the Canadians keep good records. I'll have someone run all the names: Moule, Lovelace, D'Entremont. Between Labonsky working Albuquerque and this new bit of info about Nova Scotia, maybe we'll come up with a hit. I'm going to make a few quick calls. Would you mind waiting just a few minutes?" I said I'd stay, but asked to read Hasty's file on the Lovelace murder. He pursed his lips, took a deep breath and slid the folder across the table before leaving the room and shutting the door.

The file on the murder of Penny Lovelace—no middle name—appeared to be printouts of scans from the files of the Albuquerque cold case squad or, more correctly, the Bernalillo County Sheriff's Department Cold Case Unit. There were basically three parts, the first of which were copies of Lovelace's arrest records and other encounters with the county's law enforcement and judicial system. The second contained records of the investigation of her murder, including her autopsy report, and the third consisted of current records from the cold case unit. I was immediately drawn to the oldest group dating back to 1982, when Moule would have been five or six years old. Lovelace's first encounter with the authorities occurred when she was picked up for misdemeanor possession of marijuana. The charges were apparently dropped and nothing appeared to have come of the arrest. A handwritten note seemed to imply that she was referred to a social worker. Similar encounters were documented half a dozen additional times over the following two years, including one for shoplifting—the charges were again dropped—and two for "disorderly conduct." Most notes were handwritten by the arresting officers and difficult to read.

Following an arrest in 1983, when Lovelace would have been twenty-one or twenty-two, she was again referred to a social worker, whose handwritten note was included. Though scarcely readable, the words "refuses to discuss family or life prior to recent—assume negative situation in past" were clearly legible. Her current employment—"a nightclub as waitress"— was mentioned, as well as her current living arrangements: "shares apt. w/2 other girls." Most importantly, a cryptic note near the end read "conc. re 7yo♂", then "SS ref. init." I stared at the abbreviations and symbols. In 1983, Penny Lovelace was an adult. Her life and her living arrangements, beyond any run-ins with the law, were no one's business but her own. But if she had a child, the entire picture changed. Why else would a social service consult be called? The shorthand abbreviations could be interpreted to read "concerned about seven-year-old male," referring to Lovelace's son, and "social service consult had been initiated." Whoever had written this nearly four decades earlier—the signature was illegible—was reviewing the living arrangements not only of Lovelace but also those of her minor son, the person we knew as Moule. If I was not misreading or misinterpreting the report, this opened the possibility of uncovering the facts surrounding Moule's early life—before he became Moule.

I hurriedly sifted through the remaining documents regarding Lovelace's encounters with the law prior to her murder. Beyond the 1983 note possibly referring to her son, there were no further mentions of contacts with a social worker. The records of Lovelace's murder were less revealing. By then she would have been thirty-five, and apparently well-known to law enforcement. A scanned photo of her—taken when she was in her mid-twenties—revealed a thin blonde with long hair and delicate features standing with a group of girls on a beach. A handwritten caption read "Galveston Beach—1986." The autopsy photos were gruesome. I only glanced at them before returning the images to the folder. The more recent records of the cold case unit and the DNA results confirmed what Labonsky and Hasty had already shared with me.

Hasty was gone for nearly twenty minutes, returning with an apology for taking so long. "I'm sorry—I had to call Washington to get things started on the inquiries to Canada. Law enforcement on both sides of the border get along really well, but since it's international, a lot of paperwork and the like has to be done at the outset. The plan is to first screen public record databases in the entire province of Nova Scotia for the three names I mentioned and, depending on what we come up with, go from there. It will take a week or more at the very least, I suspect, before we hear anything." He paused. "Oh, I asked for a special look at any database of runaways or missing teenage girls or the like. We don't really know what became of Moule after Lovelace left Canada—assuming that is what happened."

"But I think we do," I said, and showed him what I had found in the documents sent from the Albuquerque cold case unit.

"Damn! You're good," Hasty said, sounding genuine. "I'm not familiar with the child welfare system in Arizona, but I suspect getting information about a child who was removed from a parent's custody is going to take a court order. The data is there, if that happened, but when it's a civil rather than criminal matter the rules change." He stopped suddenly, then said, "I'm sorry—I apologize. You're an attorney. You already know that."

I smiled, trying to hide my emotions. "Yeah, I do. Been there; done that." Courtesy of the legal system, I hadn't seen my own children in five years.

I had been home only about fifteen minutes when Labonsky called. "Holy crap, John! I just got off the phone with Hasty. It looks like you may have found the roadmap to get us out of this swamp we're in. I originally came out here to try to figure out which direction I should take to track down Lovelace's son, but now—thanks to you—I know where to go. I just hope someone has saved files from the '80s pertaining to foster care placement. I can pretty well guess that they haven't been digitized, and if they exist at all they're probably packed away in a warehouse somewhere. We won't know until we start digging. And Hasty's got the ball rolling on a database search in Nova Scotia. There's a lot going on." He sighed. "But it's my job to worry about that. How are things with you? No word from anybody, I take it?" He was referring to Sarah without mentioning her name.

"No, things are quiet. I honestly don't know what I should be doing. On one hand I can't help but believe I'm being tracked, or followed, or observed or something. Whoever planted the camera at my apartment, drugged me, took my photo in bed with a naked woman, and told me they'd 'be in touch' is not going to give up and walk away that easily. And I still have no idea what they're after or why they want it. And worse, after what happened to Moule, I can only imagine the lengths they might go to in order to get what they want."

There was a long silence at the other end of the line, then Labonsky said, "Yeah."

CHAPTER 20

I needed to get away, to hide, to recover, to get my thoughts and fears under control. The mental images of the whole episode with Sarah ate at my soul. Despite a little voice in the back of my mind telling me it wasn't my fault, I knew I had made a complete fool of myself. And even though she would have been lying, Sarah had not even told me her last name. I tend to draw into my shell when I'm under stress. It's my counterproductive way of protecting myself, a holdover from my turbulent childhood. But in the process, I often shut out those who care about me, who want to help. I thought about Jenna, and how I had been avoiding her. Our relationship had always been a strange one—friends and sometimes lovers, sometimes hot, sometimes less so, but always with the knowledge that we were there for one another in times of need. She had reached out to me, but I had made excuses. It was now time for me to apologize and beg her forgiveness for my asinine stupidity. I decided I would surprise her. I'd simply arrive at the company where she worked, wait quietly in the lobby as the receptionist announced my presence, then meet with Jenna in her private office. My quixotic expedition wouldn't solve any problems, but it would allow me to express my regret and reconnect with the one person who truly understood me. I decided I would go the next morning.

Claxton is roughly a one-hour drive from the gallery in Savannah. I would leave at 9:00 a.m., planning my arrival a few minutes after 10:00, when Jenna might be ready for a break. I took my car, the one I had inherited with the Liberty Street house and gallery, a fifteen-year-old Lincoln my grandmother had purchased nearly a decade before her death. Rather than take the interstate, I-16, I chose the more southernly route, a two-lane ribbon of asphalt that passed through the wilderness of the Ogeechee River swamp, then skirted the lowlands of Fort Stewart before connecting with nearly twenty-five miles of boringly straight highway through Pembroke and into Claxton. The monotony of the forest would give me a chance to get my thoughts together before meeting Jenna. I headed south on Abercorn, past the Savannah Mall, across the Little Ogeechee River, then under I-95 where the urban four-lane transitioned to a lonely country highway. The sky was blue, marred only by the contrails of jets plying the east coast flyways high above. I passed an occasional car and tractor-trailer, but the road was, for the most part, free of traffic as dappled bits of sunlight filtered through the pine and hardwood forest on either side.

Driving just above the fifty-five miles-per-hour speed limit, I noted a dark-colored sedan a couple of hundred yards behind me, seemingly maintaining a constant distance. My wariness—or paranoia—made me wonder if I was being followed. With a straight highway and no cops in sight, I sped up to sixty-five, then seventy. The car maintained its distance, evidently matching the changes in my speed. Just beyond the Ogeechee River bridge I made a sudden exit to the right, turning sharply back toward the public boat ramp to allow a good look at the car that I imagined was following me. It sped by without slowing, a large late-model Ford sedan with tinted windows. I couldn't make out the driver or any passengers. Now feeling silly, I made a U-turn at the boat ramp parking lot and pulled back onto the highway toward Pembroke. Fifteen more miles passed, my speed slowed only by the village of Ellabell before reaching another long, lonely stretch of highway. The road now paralleled a railroad track on my left with mixed farm and timberland on my right. I happened to glance in my rearview mirror just in time to see a sedan that appeared to be the color of the Ford emerging from a forest road behind me.

I sped up. The sedan did as well, rapidly closing the gap between us. I slowed to fifty miles per hour. The sedan, now only a few dozen yards behind me, did as well. I accelerated again, but the distance between us remained the same. For the first time in a long while, I felt an unbridled sense of fear. We were now on a long straight stretch of country road lined mostly by forest on both sides. No other vehicles were in sight in either direction. We cruised along in tandem at eighty, the Ford now a couple of car lengths off my rear bumper. Glancing nervously back and forth from the road to my rearview mirror, I couldn't see who was driving. Suddenly the Ford accelerated moving up rapidly on my left side, but slowing just as it came parallel to the rear of my car. With a slight jerk to the right, the front fender of the Ford bumped the left side of my vehicle just behind the rear tire. The Lincoln jerked and tried to fishtail. For a moment I thought I was lost before regaining control. Once again the Ford, still in the oncoming traffic lane, moved forward, concentrating on another attempt. I could see the driver now in my sideview mirror, his eyes focused on my vehicle, ready to move in for the kill.

Time seemed to slow down. For some strange reason I wondered if my seat belt was securely fastened. I thought about Jenna, and the obvious fact that I wouldn't get to see her and apologize. I thought about…

Just at that moment, I looked up in time to see a large white-faced Hereford bull standing in the opposite lane just ahead. The driver of the Ford, intent on maneuvering into my rear quarter panel, apparently didn't see the animal. In my mirror I spied another man in the passenger's seat frantically waving his arms. The driver's vision jerked forward. We were now only a few dozen yards away from a bull weighing nearly a ton, and traveling toward him at eighty miles an hour, more than a hundred feet a second.

The Ford driver jerked his wheel to the left. The car veered, then skidded sideways toward the animal as I zoomed past it on the other side in the opposite lane. Barely missing the bull's hindquarters, the Ford, now out of control, hit the shoulder, flipped, and began to tumble toward the tree line. It smashed topside first into a mature pine tree, almost immediately exploding into a ball of flames. The bull stood passively in the highway, turning his head with curiosity toward the now flaming mass that used to be a car. I stopped, backed up, and watched in horror from a distance. Except for the bull and my vehicle, the highway was empty as far as the eye could see. There was nothing either of us could do. A huge plume of thick black smoke stained the otherwise clear blue sky. I put my car in park, turned off the ignition, and watched the conflagration from a safe distance. After a couple of minutes I dialed 911.

In what seemed like an instant, the highway was crowded with firetrucks, Bryan County Sheriff and Georgia State Patrol vehicles, and ambulances, the latter leaving shortly when it became evident that their services were unneeded. An accident reconstruction team photographed and measured the skid marks while two state troopers interviewed me about the circumstances of the wreck. I told the truth—with some modification. I explained that I was on my way to Claxton when the Ford sedan approached me from my rear at a high rate of speed. The driver apparently decided to pass me but did not see the bull in the road until he was in the other lane about to overtake my vehicle. I speculated that he tried to merge back into the lane behind me and in the process must have jerked his wheel to the right, which explained the fresh scrapes on the left rear quarter-panel of my car. At that point he must have then hit his brakes and turned his wheel sharply to the left, which caused him to lose control and wreck. I saw no good coming out of my trying to explain that the Ford and its occupants were following me and evidently trying to cause me to wreck. One of the officers, a lieutenant, pointedly asked if I had ever seen the Ford sedan or knew the occupants—"Road rage, you know," he explained. "Sometimes you get a crazy driver who gets mad and tries to run another car off the road." I replied, quite truthfully, that I had never before seen the car or its occupants.

"Well, I don't suppose you've looked, but there's not much there to see now," the lieutenant said. "Looks like the forensics guys are going to have to try to identify the victims. The car's a rental out of Savannah. We'll get that information and try to notify the next-of-kin." He looked at his notebook and then said, "I know this is a rough thing to have to go through, Mr. O'Toole, but it looks like someone's angel was looking after you today."

If you only knew, I thought, glancing at the bull that had wandered into the field.

CHAPTER 21

It was nearly 1:30 in the afternoon by the time I made it back to the gallery. I had spent a couple of hours recounting the same sequence of events to officers of the state patrol, the Bryan County Sheriff's Department, the accident investigation team, and the medics, who insisted on examining me despite no obvious injury. Needless to say, I'd scuttled the idea of surprising Jenna. The damage to the Lincoln appeared to be fairly superficial and nonstructural, but I planned to get the car checked as soon as possible to be sure. I spent most of the nearly hour's drive back to Savannah trying to decide who I should call for help. As far as the first responders knew, the events of earlier in the morning were a tragic accident that claimed two innocent lives. Only I knew the truth: two unknown men in a rented car had tried to run me off the road.

I chose to call Labonsky. Even though he was still in Albuquerque, he could point me in the right direction. Someone, either the Savannah cops or the FBI or both, needed to know what really happened. The detective answered his phone promptly. "What's up, John? Checking in to see where we are? I think we're making some real progress…"

I cut him off. "No. Major things are happening here." I told him of the morning's events, stressing that I had not been completely candid with the details when speaking to the officers. "As far as the state patrol and Bryan County cops know, this was an accident."

"It just gets worse, doesn't it," Labonsky said. "Listen, because of the sensitive nature of this investigation, we need to let them keep thinking that. They'll do a good job of identifying the dead men. Once we have that, we can take it from there.

But we need to let Hasty know so he can alert his guys in the Bureau. Don't forget that the tentacles of this whole thing extend pretty far."

"You haven't shared that part with me," I said.

"We need to," Labonsky replied, swiftly saying, "Let me make a few quick calls, and I'll get back to you. In the meantime, watch your back. Do you have a gun, a pistol maybe, that you can carry?"

"No."

"Think about getting one. I'll be in touch." The line went dead. For the next fifteen minutes, I sat in a chair in my apartment, feeling nearly paralyzed as I tried to decide what to do. I eventually concluded that short of becoming a hermit, there was no single thing that would either protect me or add any more to solving my problems than was already being done. Looking for a distraction, I decided to take the Lincoln to a small body shop I'd used in the past to get an estimate on repairing the damage caused by the morning's vehicular assailants. I would need to pay cash for any repairs. Attempting to file insurance would raise too many questions.

The shop was a fifteen-minute drive west in the general direction of Savannah's port, located in a mixed area of warehouses, machine shops, and other skilled-labor, blue-collar businesses. The proprietor, whose name was Dan, remembered me. "Mr. O'Toole, hiya doin'? What can we do for you today?"

I explained that I had a little scrape on the back left quarter panel of my car and wanted to get an estimate and a repair, if I could afford it. "Man, you know you can. We got the best prices in town."

"I'm paying cash. No insurance."

"In that case, the price just got better," Dan said, smiling. "Let me take a look and see what we got." He paced about the

Lincoln, looking at the dents and scrapes, kneeling down and running his hand over the damaged area. "Shouldn't be too bad to fix. Before I give you a number though, I really need to put it up on the rack to be sure there's no hidden damage behind the wheel well there." He looked at the scrapes once again and asked, "How did you say you did this?"

"I didn't. Some nut tried to change lanes on the highway. The front of his car hit the back side of mine." I figured that explanation was close enough.

"Hmm," Dan said. "Gotta worry about that kind of accident. It can cause you to lose control and wreck."

"So I've heard. Guess I was just lucky," I said, keeping the irony out of my voice.

Dan drove the Lincoln into one of the bays of his shop and stood to one side while the hydraulic lift boosted the car above head level. Using a flashlight, he peered up, exploring the area under the damaged bodywork, shaking both rear tires and generally satisfying himself that the damage was superficial. Suddenly he stopped and seemed to focus on an area high up and just behind the wheel well. He called to one of his employees to bring him a ladder.

"You see something worrisome?" I asked.

"Don't know. I need to take a closer look." Mounting a short stepladder, he reached up, straining, seemingly grasping for something. After a moment he said, "Got it." He stepped down from the ladder and emerged from under the car holding a small dark object covered with mud and road dust. It appeared to be a box of sorts. "This yours?" he asked.

"What is it?"

"Dunno. It was stuck up there with a magnet. Had to pull like hell to get it off. It ain't original equipment, whatever it is."

Dan handed the object to me. It was a small box made of heavy plastic, about three inches thick, four inches wide, and five inches long. One surface held a large flat magnet. The top was hinged with a sturdy plastic latch. I popped it open as Dan watched me intently. The outer box served to protect an inner device of some sort. "Oh, I know what that is," Dan said. "That's one of them GPS tracking things. Did you know you was being tracked? You reckon yo' wife's getting suspicious maybe?"

I didn't know how to reply. "I'm divorced," I said, sounding stupid.

Dan frowned. "Oh, that's not good. Somebody's husband then? You better be careful, Mr. O'Toole."

I snapped the outer case shut as a wave of anger and fear swept over me. Glancing around the shop, I saw a workbench nearby. "Mind if I borrow one of your tools for a minute, Dan?"

"Sure," he replied, sounding somewhat uncertain.

I walked over to the bench, selected a medium-sized ball-peen hammer from the tool rack, placed the tracking device on an anvil and proceeded to smash it into tiny pieces as Dan watched in amazement. "You really do have an anger, Mr. O'Toole," he said.

"Sometimes, if you push me far enough," I said, smiling. Changing the subject, I continued, "I really need to get home. I want to get my car fixed for sure, but finding this…this whatever-it-is changes things. How about calling me when you work up your estimate? I think you still have my phone number."

Back at my apartment I called Labonsky again. "Hey," he said without giving me a chance to tell him why I was calling, "I was just about to call you. I got in touch with Jim Hasty and filled him in. My partner, Pete Marsh, is aware of the situation with the wreck and is following up on that. I have no idea when we'll have IDs for the dead guys. But let me tell you some good news." Labonsky's speech was pressured. He was clearly excited about something. "We have a break on Penny Lovelace's son, or the person we assume is or was her son, and it's all because you picked up on the social service referral from the 1983 arrest, when he would have been six or seven years old. It took a bit of sweet-talking the lady in charge of records, but we're getting somewhere now. She was willing to confirm that the son of Penny Lovelace, a six-year-old named Donald Clarence Lovelace, was removed from his mother's custody on order of the courts and placed in Arizona's foster care system. That's just an overview, all I could get for a start, but she's working on getting formal permission for me to review the case file. Assuming we're talking about the same kid, we now have a name and a way to trace him, as he would have technically been a ward of the state of Arizona until he turned eighteen, unless someone adopted him, and even then—"

"Rod," I interrupted.

He seemed taken aback. "Yeah? I was trying to fill you in on the…"

"I know. But I called to tell you something important as well."

"Oh, I'm sorry."

"There was a tracking device hidden in my car. That's how the guys in the Ford knew where I was. They planned to kill me." There was silence from the other end of the line. "It was destroyed," I said, without adding other details.

123

CHAPTER 22

I had not been spending much time in the gallery, obviously distracted by everything else that was going on. My plans to apologize to Jenna forgotten for the moment, and with both Labonsky and Hasty confident of making progress with the investigation, I decided I should try to resume some sense of order in my life by showing up for work at the usual time and trying to pretend that all was well. So I did. When Jessica arrived at work at nine the next morning, I was in my office going over the bills and usual paperwork that every business seems to generate. "Hey. It's good to see you here," she said, sounding genuine. "You've been out of touch a lot lately."

"Yeah, I've had a bunch on my mind. I need to get back on my routine."

"Good. We've missed you—I've missed you—and we need you here," Jessica said, smiling. She closed my office door as she headed back to the front of the gallery.

I was just about to dive into the monthly financial report when my cell phone chirped in my pocket. I looked at the number—Labonsky—and answered with a wary "Hello."

"Great news," the detective said. "I got a call about nine last night from the lady in charge of the social service records archive here in Albuquerque. I didn't want to bother you so late, so I'm calling first thing this morning. She checked with the powers-that-be and has received permission to share the paperwork on the Lovelace kid who we think is Moule. Normally, we'd need to file a request and possibly have a hearing, but since this is a murder investigation and the FBI's involved, they're willing to forego all the bureaucratic crap. It's just after seven here. I'm meeting her at the archives in a couple of hours.

I hope I'll have something to report by this afternoon. I called Hasty and Marsh late last night to fill them in and told them I'd be calling you this morning." Labonsky paused, waiting for my response.

"That's good to hear," I said, silently wishing Moule had never walked into my gallery.

"And there's more. Hasty said he was making progress with the Canadians. He got in contact with someone in the Halifax RCMP—that's the FBI equivalent up there—and they agreed to do a records search for a start. That's the quick and easy part. If they come up with anything, someone will need to do some deeper digging. I asked him to keep you in the loop."

We talked for a few more minutes before ending the call. Maybe I would have a break for a few days while the investigation ground on. I had no sooner started back studying the monthly financials when my cell chirped again. The number was Jenna's. "Are you okay?" she said, her voice an octave higher and full of concern.

"Yes, sure. Why are you asking?" She couldn't have known about the accident—or did she?

"The wreck yesterday, near Pembroke. There was something about it on the radio this morning. I heard it on the way to work. Two men got killed. They mentioned that someone named O'Toole from Savannah gave a statement to the police, and I thought it couldn't be you because you would have told me about it if you were coming this way, but then I started worrying and…"

Interrupting her, I lied, "Yeah, I heard that, too. I don't know who that was, but I'm okay." Jenna gave an audible sigh of relief. "Listen," I continued, "I owe you an apology. I've been under a lot of stress with this Moule thing and I know I've been kinda distant and maybe even avoiding—"

"Hey," Jenna said. "I understand. It's all right. I'm here when you need me. Nothing's changed. I love you." For an instant I didn't know what to say. "Okay?" she asked.

"Okay," I replied, feeling a bit choked up.

"We'll get things back on track when this storm blows over." She hung up without waiting for my reply.

The remainder of the day passed quietly, at least until five o'clock. I ate lunch at a nearby deli, something I had been accustomed to doing fairly regularly before Moule. The waitress commented that she had not seen me in a while and wanted to know if everything was all right. "Just great," I replied. I was getting accustomed to lying. "Work's been keeping me busy." She opined that was good.

Just before five Hasty called. "Bingo!" he said, sounding excited. "We got a hit, in fact, I think we may have found the key—at least part of it—to Moule's history. The guy I've been talking with in Halifax said he thought the best way to start was to run the three names we know, Moule, D'Entremont, and Lovelace, against a list of missing persons. Well, he got a match almost immediately: a twenty-year-old mother and her five-year-old son were put on the register in March 1981. She'd had several run-ins with the law and had been threatened with the loss of custody of her child. At the time, she was apparently on her own. Her parents kicked her out when she turned eighteen. I get the impression that no one suspected foul play, but rather that she'd absconded to avoid losing custody of the kid. She was an adult, and if he hadn't been in the picture I don't think anyone would have called the authorities. The match was a hit in the database because of her name, Penelope Marie D'Entremont."

"You're kidding?" I found myself grinning.

"Not at all," Hasty said, "but there's more. Back in those

days it would have been pretty easy to enter the US from Canada as, say, a day visitor. Minimal paperwork, no visas, none of that. And if she had a kid with her, that would be all the more reason to think she'd be returning home. She probably planned it all along—leave the snow and ice of Halifax, head south to the warmth of the American Southwest, change your name and start a new life. But from what we now know, it looks like not a lot changed. She ended up losing custody of her kid anyway. Now we need to find out what happened to him—to Moule—after that. I feel certain Rod will come up with something from the archives in Albuquerque."

"This is great. The light at the end of the tunnel," I said.

"I wish," Hasty said. "Don't forget we've got other concerns. That's why the Bureau put me on the case. I honestly think we're just getting started." I felt like he'd thrown a bucket of cold water on my rising hopes.

"I guess we'll just have to see," I said before hanging up.

One of my great flaws is my tendency to overthink things: relationships, situations, the motivations of people I interact with, and the like. It's something I recognized in my early twenties, a penchant for analysis when none is needed or appropriate. Initially, I blamed it on law school and the necessity of understanding the intricacies of the law and the circumstances of its applications. I told myself I should just relax and let Labonsky and Hasty and the rest of the team do their jobs. After all, it seemed they were making progress. If what I had learned during the day was correct, Moule's history was about to be revealed. It should now be a simple matter to trace his background, his associates, and how and why he ended up in Savannah wanting to buy investment-grade art. But as before, the more I thought about it, the more complex the problem became. What about Sarah? What did she and whomever she was working with want from me? Who were the two men—now dead—who tried to run me off the road, and why? The unverified assumption was that these events were in some unknown way related to Moule's murder. Thus far, there was nothing at all to connect the three situations. I felt an urgent desire to consume a large glass of bourbon. Instead, I headed home to an empty apartment and a frozen dinner heated in my microwave.

CHAPTER 23

Labonsky called again late the next afternoon. He had spent the day at the warehouse where the social service records from the 1980s were stored, eagerly assisted by one of the record librarians. "She said she'd never helped out on a real murder investigation," the detective said. "I got all I think we'll need. A timeline, school records, periodic reports from caseworkers and so forth. Back then, Moule was known as 'Don' Lovelace. He was lucky in that he was placed the entire time with just one family, the Spires, who raised him under the foster care program until he turned eighteen and graduated from high school. Those are just the high points; they copied and printed out the whole folder for me. It's about two and a half inches thick. I've got a flight back to Atlanta first thing tomorrow morning, with a two-hour layover before I make the connection to Savannah. I'll use the time to read all this paperwork and maybe decide what direction we need to take next.

"And another thing," Labonsky continued, "the sketch artist guy called. He said he thinks he's figured out the tattoo on this Sarah person. I don't know if that's important, but we don't want to miss anything. You know, it finally seems like all this is coming together."

Labonsky sounded confident as he ended the call. I wasn't so sure. Neither of us, nor anyone else, had yet to say how Sarah and the two dead men fit into the puzzle.

As if someone could read my thoughts, at that moment my cell phone rang. The screen message read "Unknown Caller." I hesitated, then flipped it open and said "Hello."

"Hi, John," a chillingly familiar voice said. "It's Sarah. I hope you don't mind my calling you."

"I'm listening," I said, my voice harsh. "Talk."

"I'm sorry about the other night," Sarah said, her voice soft and soothing. "I guess you made it home without too many problems." She waited for my response, but when I did not reply, she continued. "And I'm sorry about someone trying to cause you to wreck. We had nothing to do with that, although we're pretty sure who's responsible. Two of their better people are dead, so please be careful. They may try again. Or may not; we don't know." She paused again, then said, "Are you still listening?"

"I am," I said.

"You have something we want. Something that rightfully belongs to us. We want it back. You may be recording this call, so I'm not going to say what it is. We assume you know, and know how to recover it, even if you won't admit it. You talked to me—to us—for a while the other night after you passed out—you probably don't remember it. You kept denying that Moule had passed it on to you, but we are sure he did. We could have killed you then, but we did not. There would be no sense in that, and it wouldn't accomplish anything. We mean you no harm so long as you cooperate with us."

"I have no idea what you're talking about," I said.

"I don't believe you, but I can understand why you wouldn't want to admit it. But there are other people—our enemies—who also know you have it. They want it, too. And if they can't get their hands on it, they are obviously willing to kill you to prevent us from having it. So you see, it puts both of us in a bad spot. If you work with us, all will be fine. If not, well…" Sarah left the sentence unfinished. "Why don't you think about it for a day or two? We'll keep in touch." With a click, the call ended.

My first reaction was to call someone—Labonsky, Hasty,

even Holloway on his European cruise. But that's what I always seemed to do. Something happens and I pick up the phone and whine to someone. Enough handholding. In the general scheme of things Sarah's call meant nothing. Other than the fact that the two unfortunate men who tried to kill me ended up dead themselves thanks to karma in the form of a Hereford bull, nothing had changed. I planned to mention the call next time I saw one of the investigators.

Pete Marsh called two days later asking if I could meet with the group that afternoon. Both Labonsky and Hasty wanted to go over what they had discovered, and they wanted my thoughts on Sarah's tattoo. I told him I knew nothing of tattoos, to which he replied, "We don't either, but that's not the point. We'll talk about it when you get here."

At four o'clock I found myself sitting in the now-familiar police headquarters conference room with Labonsky, Hasty, and Marsh. Hasty took the lead. "John, as I'm sure you've figured out, what started as the investigation of a murder has merged with an ongoing federal investigation, which is why I've been assigned here. You are the one person we know in this city who had contact with the man we call Moule before his murder, the only person he talked with and shared some of his background. You've been cooperative and have made some important contributions to the case, but for reasons I'm sure you understand, we've not been able to share everything with you. I've talked about this with the guys above me at the Bureau, and I've received permission on a federal level to share the details of the case, why we are interested in Moule, and why his murder makes it even more important that we bring this investigation, this case, to a satisfactory conclusion." Hasty looked at Labonsky and Marsh; both nodded in agreement. "So let me give you a quick overview from my perspective and then we can get on discussing what we've come up with in Nova Scotia and Albuquerque.

"Prior to his death," Hasty continued, "we had Moule on our radar as a rising star in cryptocurrency trading. The guy was clearly brilliant, and while there's nothing illegal about what he was doing, the folks he was working with were on our watch list as potential national security threats. I'll leave it at that for the moment. We think he was killed because of some dispute over money, but we have no real idea about any details. The reason the bad guys—plus a whole lot of normal, God-fearing, law-abiding Americans—are into cryptocurrency is that the transactions are effectively anonymous. Unlike conventional stock trading, or currency trading for that matter, no one, including the state or federal governments or the IRS, knows what's going on. What if, for example, a domestic terrorist group needs funding? Trading cryptocurrency is the ideal way to avoid detection. What we're looking for now is anything that will help us connect Moule to his clients, data that was missing and possibly taken from his home and office when you discovered his body. We know that the day before he was killed he transferred millions of dollars offshore, beyond our ability to trace it. The question is why. And who has access to those funds now? That's what we want to know."

"In addition to who killed Moule," Labonsky added, citing the obvious.

"Yeah, sorry," Hasty said. "Guess we're focusing on different aspects of the case. But I think if we get the answer to one, we'll have the answer to both."

Labonsky took over. "Okay, let's go over what we've found and decide what direction we should take." For the next fifteen minutes he recounted in detail his trip to Albuquerque and what he had discovered about the decade Moule spent with the Spires, his foster family, when he was known as Don Lovelace. The copies of his social services record indicated that he was a good student, making mostly A's, that he was a member of his middle and high school computer clubs, and that his teachers' and social workers' comments uniformly described him as "shy" and having "poor social skills." The latter did not seem surprising given his childhood before being removed from his mother's custody. "Besides a copy of his file, they also gave me these," Labonsky said, pointing to a small stack of bound books. "Actually, they loaned them to me and I'm supposed to send them back. They're the yearbooks—the 'annuals' they call them—for Moule's four years of high school. I didn't have time to look at them and thought maybe you might, John. I'm not sure what more we'll learn."

Hasty briefly went over what he had learned from his contacts in Halifax. "I don't think there's much pertinent there. Moule's mother, Penelope D'Entremont, left when she was pretty young. Most of what's important seemed to happen after she arrived in New Mexico. Do you have any questions thus far, John?"

"Not now," I said.

"Okay, then, let's see what your artist guy has to say about the tattoo," Hasty said, nodding at Marsh, who left briefly and returned with a slim young man whose peroxide blond hair was streaked with shades of green and magenta. "This is Chet Hartley, our artist-in-residence," Marsh said, adding, "He's a graduate of SCAD," as if this might explain the hair color. Labonsky rolled his eyes, thinking no one was looking.

"Well," Hartley began. "You gave me a real assignment this time. Not some boring listen-to-the-witness-and-draw-the-perp job. And it was interesting. I think I've figured out what this naked person's tattoo is." Holding up the original enlarged photo of Sarah's tattoo, he said, "This is what you gave me to start with. As you can see, it appears to be part of a square tattoo, with a field of green ink on the top and bottom, and seven lines—alternating black and white stripes really. Just at the far edge where the rest of the tattoo can't be seen, the lines seem to run into a white circle bounded in black lines. Inside that, there's what appears to be a 'K,' maybe the last letter in a word.

"My first thought," Hartley continued, "was that square tattoos are kinda unusual. I won't tell you all the time I spent imagining what it might be, but the possibility of this being part of a flag popped into my mind—I have a close friend who has a flag tattooed on his upper back, and when you see him with his shirt off the end of it sort of looks like this." Labonsky smirked. "Well, I started looking at flag designs and came up with this." He handed out prints of a flag divided into four

quadrants by black lines resembling the design on Sarah's tattoo. Each quadrant was bright red instead of green. The lines intersected in a circle, like Sarah's, inside of which was a swastika. The upper left quadrant of the flag displayed a Maltese cross. "This, gentlemen, is the World War II flag of the German Wehrmacht—the military." He gave everyone a moment to examine the image before continuing. "But that flag is primarily red. I think the tattoo on this person's back is part of this." Hartley handed out a second image, this of a flag that in its general layout resembled the Nazi flag, but with green quadrants instead of red and an abstract symbol inside in the inner circle. "This is the flag of Kekistan."

Hasty slammed his fist on the table. "Dammit, I knew it!"
Hartley beamed. The rest of us stared blankly at the images.

CHAPTER 24

"And just what the hell is Kekistan?" Labonsky asked, a hint of antagonism in his voice.

Hartley smiled. "Well, it doesn't really exist. You see…," he began, only to be cut off by Hasty.

"I'll answer that, Rod." Turning to Hartley he said, "Thank you, Chet. That is going to be a real help." The artist flashed another smile at Labonsky and scurried out of the conference room.

Labonsky stared at the table sullenly. Marsh said, "What was that all about? And yeah, what or who is Kekistan?"

"It could be the link that helps us to put this all together," Hasty replied. "And by the way, I had no idea until just now what Hartley had come up with. It's as much of a surprise to me as it is to you, but once you understand it, you'll appreciate its meaning." He glanced at his watch. "We're spending too damn much time in this conference room talking about the case. We need to be out doing fieldwork and digging for answers. But with that said, let me quickly review why the Bureau assigned me as the liaison. John, a lot of what I want to say is for your education. Pete, Rod, you've probably heard most of this before, but since you don't seem to know about this flag and its meaning, I'm going to quickly review things. Okay?" The three of us signaled our agreement.

"I think all of us would agree that we live in a great country. Most Americans consider themselves patriots. They respect the flag and they love mom, home, and apple pie. That doesn't mean they approve of everything that goes on politically, or respect all of what the government does sometimes, or like all of our leaders and politicians. The one thing we depend on and know, however, is that the citizens, the American people, the voters, are ultimately in charge. Change is possible and happens every several years with elections at all levels of government. Our rights are laid out specifically in the Constitution and its amendments. All of us in this room—including you, John—took an oath at one time to defend them.

"And our rights to speak our minds and engage in peaceful protests are protected by the First Amendment, as you well know. You can carry signs and picket, protest in the streets, give speeches, post things on social media, or pay for ads on TV. You can't do that in most other countries; in much of the rest of the world you'll end up in jail—or worse. But sometimes in our own country, some folks get the belief that more than simple incremental change is needed, that America is rotten to the core, that wiping the slate clean politically and starting over is the only solution. That's what the communists did in Russia and China, what the Nazis tried to do in Europe—it goes on and on.

"Well, here in the US, there are groups that would destroy the American system. There always have been. Back in the first part of the twentieth century, for example, there was the anarchist movement with its bombings and assassinations. More recently we have the likes of Timothy McVeigh and the Oklahoma City bombing that killed 168 people, including 19 kids. We all know groups like this are active in this country at this very moment. And my job—no, our job—is to stop them." Hasty hesitated, looking at each of us in turn for our reactions, thinking perhaps that he had become too forceful in his rhetoric.

"I think you're preaching to the choir, Jim," Labonsky said, speaking with a tone of frustration tinged with hostility.

"How about explaining how this Kek-something flag is related to this investigation, and to Moule in particular. We all know that there are a bunch of bad guys out there—gangs, the mob, conspiracies and what have you, but you gotta remember, this is a murder investigation. I don't think hearing about anarchists and stuff that happened a hundred years ago has much to do with anything. I know that's the Bureau's national priority, but this is a Savannah murder, so let's cut to the bottom line."

Hasty seemed taken aback, looking down and initially not responding to the outburst. After an awkward pause, he said, "I guess you're right. I'm sorry, it's just that my job is to see the bigger picture." Picking up the folder with images of Sarah's tattoo and the flags, he continued, "I'll keep this brief. Most groups that represent a national security threat are driven by an agenda. Islamic terrorists, for example, believe Western society is decadent and immoral and want to destroy it rather than convince nonbelievers that their way is best. In such struggles, symbols become important—that's why they targeted the World Trade Center, the US Capitol, and the Pentagon on September 11th. There are many others—the Ku Klux Klan burns crosses. The swastika has become a powerful hate symbol—it's illegal in many European countries but not in the US. Some of the most powerful symbols are flags. We rally around the stars and stripes, but some white-supremist groups have adopted the Confederate battle flag.

"Assuming Hartley is correct about this person's tattoo representing this flag"—Hasty picked up the image of the green and black-striped banner—"and assuming it's not a tattoo she got and regretted, she may be a member or follower of one of several right-wing groups whose agendas revolve around what they refer to as the 'preservation of Western civilization,' built on the core beliefs of white supremacy and all that goes with that, including such things as closed borders, rejection of non-Christian religions, and suppression of individual rights of whole classes of American citizens. As to the flag, it had its origin in the video game world, specifically the Warcraft games that date back nearly twenty years or so. What they taught us at the Academy was that the flag and name of the fictious country of Kekistan became popular among a certain group of gamers and later became a secret sign indicating political views." Hasty stopped, looking at each of us in turn. "Any questions?" No response. "Okay, then. This gives me a place to start from the perspective of the Bureau. I need to make a few calls." With that he turned and left the room, shutting the door forcefully behind him.

After a difficult moment of silence, Marsh said, "He's not happy."

"I think not," Labonsky agreed.

I remained silent.

"Well," Labonsky said, "we need to get back to work." He turned to me. "John, if there's nothing else we need to discuss, I'd appreciate you looking at these yearbooks from Moule's— I'm sorry, Lovelace's—high school years and letting me know if there's anything you see that may be important." Gesturing toward Marsh, he added, "Pete, let's see what we can find out about the two guys that got killed in the wreck."

With the four Albuquerque High School yearbooks in hand, I left police headquarters feeling somewhat uneasy and a little confused. Labonsky's outburst at Hasty was harsh, especially considering that they were two cops supposedly working toward the same goal. But then I could see how Labonsky might resent the FBI sending in an agent to get involved in the case. Labonsky was the lead detective on a murder case. Hasty's agenda centered on following up on national security interests, looking for whatever connection Moule might have had in helping fund what he called "domestic terrorists." Maybe this was just the way things worked. I wasn't sure.

CHAPTER 25

Back at my apartment, I eagerly dove into the four books from Moule's high school years when he was known as Don Lovelace. Labonsky was probably correct; I doubted I would learn anything useful regarding his murder or, for that matter, anything else in the case. My interest was one of simple curiosity. Opening the first yearbook, I had no problem finding the ninth-grade photo of Donald Clarence Lovelace. Among the pages of other students whose last name began with an "L," Moule's plump round face, framed by dark longish hair and adorned by a pair of black-rimmed glasses, was instantly recognizable. He did not smile, either in that photo or in the other three headshots from his sophomore, junior, or senior years. Among the dedications and awards, the photos of smiling "most-likely-to-succeeds" and class officers, Moule was nowhere to be found. There were other, unnamed images of him. In the "Clubs and Organizations" section he appeared each year on the front row of the Bulldog Computer Club—the Bulldog being the school's mascot. In a group shot of the Beta Club, whose membership was predicated on having consistent listing on the school's Honor Roll for grades, Lovelace/Moule was again present in each of the four years. The only photos in which he displayed a smile—or any sort of discernable emotion—were found in the yearbooks for his junior and senior years. In both volumes he was shown grinning at the camera while sitting in front of a desktop computer of 1990s vintage with a huge CRT screen. The caption below one image read, "Don Lovelace, better known by his gaming handle as 'DC,' is founder and president of the Bulldog Gamers, Albuquerque High's Digital Warriors." About a dozen unnamed kids of the same age beamed at the camera from behind the desk. This confirmed what Moule had mentioned to me about his addiction to the "fantasy worlds" of video games, as he called them.

Pete Marsh dropped by the gallery early the next morning. "Labonsky's off for the day, so I thought I'd come by and see your gallery," he said. The excuse sounded hollow. After a few pleasantries and a cup of coffee he admitted, "Look, the real reason I came by was that I was kind of embarrassed by Rod's comments to Hasty yesterday. That's not like him. Normally he's a pretty nice guy, but more than anything else he's a professional and acts like one. But he's been under a lot of stress lately. His wife left him a while back, and from what little he's told me, she's got it in her mind that she's going to take everything he's got. She's hired some lawyer who's milking her dry in legal fees to help her do just that. The wife took their car, and Rod's been having to make do with the old truck…"

"Hey, I've been there," I said. "I know what he's going through."

"Well, you understand then. Their kids are grown and gone, and all Rod's got now is his work. He puts in twelve-hour days to keep his mind off the divorce, and maybe to make a little overtime. The wife went to court and got temporary support, so he's having to pay for two households. Rod says he really needs the money. He took personal leave today to meet with his lawyer; that's part of the reason I came by.

"But I also wanted to bring you up to speed on the two guys killed in the wreck. After the crash and the fire there wasn't much left of either one of them, nothing that would let the forensics guys come up with a quick ID. But the car was a rental, and that turned out to be the key. It was paid for with a stolen and cloned credit card. The guy who rented it had what seemed to be a valid Alabama driver's license. It was a fake, too, but"—Marsh grinned—"thanks to technology, they think they've got the guy's name. The rental agency has a policy of having their agents look at the driver's license photo to be sure it's of the person renting the vehicle, then after that they scan an image of the license into their system. What the bad guys don't count on is facial recognition technology. With a little bit of pressure from Hasty, the FBI was able to speed things up and identify the driver based on his photo. His name was Roger Crutchfield, originally from Charlottesville, Virginia. He was thirty-eight and has a long criminal record dating back to his teen years, which means he had a number of mug shots in the system. He got involved with gangs during one of his stints in prison, and most recently has been an active member of the Bunker Hill Militia, an anti-government, survivalist group centered in northern Alabama and eastern Tennessee. They show up at protests all over the East Coast, mostly condemning the government while hiding behind the First Amendment. The group's been suspected of funding their operations through several bank robberies, but they've managed to get away clean thus far."

"So the FBI has a name. What can they do?" I asked.

"Basically nothing, not until someone is actually caught breaking the law, or planning something illegal."

"But this guy tried to kill me."

"I believe you, and as far as I know so does everyone else involved in the case. But think about it. The men that supposedly attacked you are dead. There are no witnesses, and whatever evidence might have existed was destroyed by the fire. Yeah, the car rental agency might have a case against their estates, but..." Marsh didn't finish the sentence. His point was obvious. "Besides you, the only living, breathing person we know who has a link to any of this is the Sarah person who—"

"She called me," I said.

Marsh sat up suddenly in his chair. "What did you just say?"

"I said she called me."

"When? Why? What did she want?" I repeated the details of our conversation to Marsh. "Well, why the hell didn't you say anything? Why didn't you tell everyone yesterday that she'd called?" he demanded.

"I was going to, but if you remember, we got distracted with the spat between Hasty and Labonsky."

"Hmm, yeah," Marsh said, "but you said she mentioned some other folks who are also chasing whatever her people are after, right?" I nodded. "And both groups must be thinking you know something or have something valuable and you're holding out on them by saying you don't know what they're talking about?"

"Right," I said.

Marsh appeared to be organizing his thoughts for a brief moment and then said, "I know it's a long shot, but this may be very important. If we know that the dead man, Crutchfield, is a member of this group, the Bunker Hill Militia, and if Sarah's tattoo connects her to one or more other groups in the same general category, maybe the feds can help us come up with a strategy, a plan to get closer to finding out what they're looking for, and from there maybe discovering who killed Moule and why."

"I have a couple of other ideas," I said. "This quarrel between Labonsky and Hasty is not helping the progress of the investigation. It looks to me like a turf battle. Labonsky's the lead detective, and he's focusing on Moule's murder; Hasty seems far more interested in the bigger picture and whatever national security implications it might have. You guys have had this case for months, and I don't think you're much closer to figuring it out than you were when you started." Marsh listened intently. "You've got a murder and no firm suspects. The feds think one or more groups with ideological agendas are in-volved—domestic terrorists and that sort. But here in Savan-nah you're looking at it mainly as a homicide. In chasing down leads, you've been following standard protocol: you start with the crime scene and whichever witnesses or other evidence you can come up with, then chase down each lead until you find what you're looking for, right?" Marsh gave a slight nod. "How about starting from a different direction?"

"What do you mean?" Marsh asked.

"Get the bad guys to show you the way," I said.

Marsh frowned. "You gotta explain that."

"Okay. Moule had something that Sarah said belonged to whatever group she's working with. Logically that had to be something of value, either cash he had invested for them or something that could be converted to cash. When she called me, she made several things clear: Moule was in possession of the missing something before he died. She thinks he passed it to me, and now I have it or have access to it. Her opposition doesn't want her group to get it back. They were willing to kill me to prevent that."

"We know all that, so what are you getting at?"

"Two things. I wait for Sarah to call me again, and when she does I set up a meeting with her. I can lie and tell her I know what she's looking for, and that I want a piece of the action if I get it back to her. I can wear a wire and have you guys hiding nearby if things start to go bad. She may not have permission to negotiate with me and may need to talk with someone else before agreeing to any deal. No matter what, I think I'll be safe, because supposedly I am the only person who knows where the money is—again assuming we're talking about money. Or cryptocoins or gold or diamonds..."

Marsh cut me off, "And what was the second thing?"

"You guys have made a lot of progress in finding out about Moule's past. We know about Canada and Albuquerque and his high school years. But then there's a gap of several years when we don't know anything. We pick up his story again after Don Lovelace has become Donald D'Entremont Moule and ends up with a PhD. What happened during those missing years? Who were Lovelace's friends before he changed his name, and why did he do it? During his last two years in high school, he was the founder and president of a school club of gamers—computer geek types. There are a couple of group photos of the members, about a dozen in all each year. We have no information at all about his friends, guys or gals he hung out with. If we follow up on those things, we may find connections that lead to his murderer."

CHAPTER 26

Marsh said he would run my ideas past Labonsky and Hasty. "Getting some more information out of Sarah sounds pretty solid—we're not making much headway doing what we've been doing." I told him I'd compare the yearbook photos of the kids in the Bulldog Gamers to the class photos and see if I could come up with a list of names of DC Lovelace's friends. I didn't have high expectations of finding something of significance, but at this point it seemed that any little thing might be important.

Identifying the other members of the Bulldog Gamers was surprisingly easy. Besides Lovelace/Moule, there were eleven students in the photo for his junior year and twelve for his senior year. Nine of the group were the same in both years, which meant I had to assign names to fourteen different kids, including five girls and nine boys, most with longish hair that made gender choices slightly challenging. After a brief half-hour search, I'd managed to find the names of thirteen students in the group. I scanned in the photos from the yearbook, then scribbled the known names under the images on copies. On a separate sheet I typed a list of the names, planning to give copies to both Hasty and Labonsky for follow-up as they saw fit. I presumed Marsh would pass on my suggestions to the two of them, but didn't know when or if they'd get back to me. I scanned everything into a single document and printed out copies for the detectives.

Just as I was finishing up, Phil Holloway called. "Hey, John! We're back, all refreshed and ready to go. I'm going to spend the day at the office tomorrow catching up, then it's back to the grind. I haven't heard much from you, so I presume things are going smoothly?" The slight rising inflection at the end of his sentence posed a question.

"Well," I began, "since we last went over the details, we've tracked down Moule's background except for a few years between high school and when he started college. And on a personal basis I've been drugged and photographed in bed with a naked woman, presumably to blackmail me, have found out I had tracking devices in my phone and car, and had two guys try to kill me by running me off the highway, but thanks to a Hereford bull in the road, they wrecked instead and were burned up when their gas tank exploded. And those are just the headlines."

Holloway burst out laughing. "One thing I like about you, John, is your sense of humor. Heck, I've only been gone two weeks. How could anyone cram all that into fourteen days? Next thing, you're going to be talking about some vast conspiracy…"

"That, too," I said. "I'm serious, Phil."

"No," he said softly, then listened quietly as I went over the events of the preceding weeks, starting with my meeting Sarah and ending with Lovelace/Moule's high school yearbooks. "What do you want me to do?" Holloway asked. "I've got your back, at least from a legal standpoint, but it looks like they've made you part of the investigation team."

"Yeah, right now I think I'm okay. The next steps involve following up on Moule's missing years and waiting to see if Sarah gets in touch with me again." I didn't mention that I hoped to meet with her in order to get a lead on who she was working with or for. Holloway would have told me I was a fool, but at this point I didn't care. We ended the conversation promising to keep in close touch. I sealed the documents with the names of the Bulldog Gamers in an envelope and dropped it off with the detectives' secretary at police headquarters. It was now late in the day. I strolled the easy half-mile to River Street and grabbed a corned beef sandwich for supper in one of the riverfront pubs, nursing my iced tea and watching the massive cargo ships pass by.

For a brief moment in time, my situation seemed to be stable. The next two days passed uneventfully. I was at the gallery as usual, keeping busy enough with the routine of a small but generally successful business, meeting with customers and potential buyers who wandered in and out of the shop during the busy summer season. On the third day, two things happened to jerk me back to reality. First, Labonsky called to say that the FBI had identified one of Lovelace/Moule's high school acquaintances as a "former person of interest." I asked what that meant, to which the detective replied, "He got caught. He's in federal prison in Beaumont, Texas, serving a ten-year sentence for securities fraud. They didn't share all the details, but one of the agents out there is going to interview him tomorrow morning. It's not the usual thing in the federal system, but there's a possibility of maybe inducing him to talk in exchange for transfer to a less restrictive facility or the like. I don't know; that's their thing—not mine."

And Sarah called again. It was just after 5:30 in the afternoon. We had closed the gallery at five, and I was back in my apartment reading the news online and considering which of the frozen meals in my refrigerator I should eat for dinner when my cell phone buzzed. The screen message again read, "Unknown Caller." The last time it had been Sarah. I stared at the phone as a dozen thoughts flashed through my mind. I had discussed with Pete Marsh my idea about meeting with Sarah and telling her I knew how to get my hands on Moule's treasure—or whatever she was after—in hopes that our connection

149

might lead somewhere. But I didn't know if Marsh in turn had presented it to Labonsky and Hasty. In a microsecond I decided I would just have to wing it. I flipped open the phone and said, "Hello."

"Hello, John," a soft voice said.

"Hello, Sarah," I replied, speaking equally softly.

"You don't sound so hostile this time," she said. "I told you I would call. I was wondering if you had thought things over, possibly considered your options."

"Remind me what they are again," I said, hoping she would catch the sarcasm.

"Well, once more, we want to recover what is rightfully ours. We think—no, we're sure—you know what that means and have the key. You can do nothing, in which case you're going to make some dangerous people even more angry than they already are. At the very least, we're sure you wouldn't want Jenna to see the photo I sent you earlier. Or there could be a terrible accident, one that left you blind or paralyzed. That would be a sad way to live out the rest of your long life. And worst of all, you could just be strolling to dinner on River Street one evening, like you did a couple of days ago. I hear drive-by shootings—murders—happen in Savannah. They rarely, if ever, catch those responsible.

"On the other hand," Sarah continued, "you could turn it over to us. To show our appreciation we'd…well, we'd do nothing. You could live your life as if this had all been a bad nightmare. Maybe get married again. Grow old knowing your secrets are safe. Do you understand me?"

"I do."

"What are you thinking?" Sarah asked.

"Okay, I'll admit I know what you're after," I lied. "And we both know it's worth a lot."

"True," she interjected.

"So, how about a commission for me, a finder's fee, if you will? This whole ordeal—and you in particular—has put me through hell. I don't want much—say ten percent of the value."

"Ooh, that's a lot, John," Sarah said, her voice still silky smooth. "And really, why should we give you anything? By returning what's ours, we're giving you back your life and your future."

"I could tell the cops. I've been working pretty closely with them."

"So I've heard." Sarah was silent for a moment. "Tell you what. I'll discuss your request with the others. We'll take a vote and see how it turns out. I'll call you back in a few days."

"Okay."

"And John," Sarah said, "may I add a personal note?"

"Sure."

"I really find you attractive. Kind of sexy even. At the condo when I was lying there naked beside you in bed, I was getting so turned on, and—" I flipped the phone shut. I did not want to hear the rest of what she had to say.

CHAPTER 27

I was torn as to what to do about Sarah. Clearly, I couldn't trust her. Considering the investigation so far, she was a prime suspect in Moule's murder. And even if she had not pulled the trigger herself, she was an accessory. She spoke casually about the risk to my life from other people, referring to them as her "enemies." She was dangerous, there was no doubt about that. The thing that puzzled me the most, though, was her seductive nature—her comments when we first met, the photo of us in bed, her come-on just before I hung up the phone. All of this added a whole different dimension. What was Jessica's expression? "Like a moth to a flame?" I needed to think this through, but for the moment I tried to stuff the thoughts in the back of my mind.

On the other hand, the fact that the FBI had found someone who knew Lovelace/Moule in high school and was now in federal prison for securities fraud appeared to have real potential for shedding light on the important years before Don Lovelace, high school geek and gaming nerd, became Don Moule, whose career would lead to vast wealth and eventually to his murder. Labonsky said the Texas federal prisoner, whose name was Arturo Gutiérrez, seemed eager to cooperate. He, Hasty, and Marsh had prepared and emailed a list of specific questions relating to the investigation, including an image of the flag that appeared to be represented in Sarah's tattoo. The Texas agent promised to send a video of the interview as soon as possible.

To my surprise, Labonsky called shortly after lunch the next day. One of the agents from the FBI's Beaumont field office had interviewed Gutiérrez that morning and would be emailing a video copy for the Savannah cops to review. "We should have it downloaded by five. You want to meet us at headquarters and watch it? I think you should. This was pretty much your idea." I said I'd be there.

Shortly after 5:00 p.m. I was sitting in a large video-equipped conference room with Labonsky, Marsh, Hasty, and four others who had been involved in the Moule case since the start of the investigation. The only one of the four I had met was Chet Hartley, the rainbow-haired sketch artist. Hasty explained that he had invited him because something came up in the interview about the flag tattoo, but I suspected he did so in part to annoy Labonsky. As the interview was done by an FBI agent, Hasty was in charge. "This video lasts just over an hour, so I hope you all don't mind sitting through it. I haven't seen it, of course, but from what the agent told me, this may be important. So make yourselves comfortable. I think we should watch it through before we start discussing the details. You each have a legal pad in front of you, and the video has a digital time stamp displayed at the bottom of the screen if you want to jot down something that needs to be reviewed later." Seeing that everyone was agreeable, Hasty dimmed the lights and pressed a few buttons on a remote. A beam from an overhead projector illuminated a screen that filled the wall at one end of the room.

For the next hour and a half, we watched in fascination as the FBI agent interviewed the prisoner Gutiérrez, stopping the video several times to replay specific sections. To me, it seemed that maybe the pieces of a huge, complex jigsaw puzzle were beginning to fall into place. The interview was done in a well-lighted room with a window just out of camera view. The prisoner, wearing a bright orange jumpsuit, sat on one side of a moderately sized table facing the agent who sat opposite him. There were two cameras, one giving an overall view from one end of the table, while the other, which could be seen as an inset in the larger picture, focused on the prisoner's face, providing a clear view of his expressions and reactions as the two men talked. The mood was generally friendly; Gutiérrez seemed eager to talk, obviously hoping his cooperation would lead to some unspecified benefits.

The prisoner was a handsome olive-skinned man who appeared to be in his mid-forties, about Moule's age. His dark hair and small moustache were neatly trimmed, and he spoke with a barely perceptible Hispanic accent. After the appropriate onscreen introductions for the record and the stated assurance that he was speaking voluntarily and had received no inducements or rewards for his testimony, the interview began. Gutiérrez said he and "Don Lovelace" had become friends in the eighth grade, each having an interest in the then-relatively new field of personal computers. "I mean it was weird, you know," Gutiérrez said, "me a guy straight out of the *barrio,* and him a fat little nerdy kid. He kinda saw something in me that nobody else did. We became bros, man. We were both into computers and games and stuff. I guess you could say I was probably his best friend until he decided to kinda drop everything and change his life."

The FBI agent, whose name was Smith, asked, "Did you know him when he decided to change his name and go back to school?"

"Oh, yeah, of course. And we kept up for the longest time until he decided to move somewhere—Savannah, Georgia, I think it was. I mean we was friends and all, but he sorta went in one direction and I went in the other." Gutiérrez paused, biting his lip. "You see, we was both into gaming back then. I mean, like, we was spending a lot of the day online, playing games competitively. And we were good, super good, especially in the Warcraft games, which was just getting started back then. Hey, have you ever been into video games, Mr. Smith?"

Smith shook his head and said, "No."

"Well, let me tell you, it's great. I guess you've never heard of 'DC Lovelace' then? No? He was the king, the champ, the one that everybody wanted to be. He was smarter, faster, and foxier than just about anybody. If you were online—especially in a first-person-shooter game—you did not want to see DC's avatar coming at you, 'cause if you did, you was toast."

"So Lovelace was successful as a gamer after high school? How long did that last?" Smith asked.

"Ah…I don't remember exactly. Several years, I'd say. He was making a good living with paid endorsements and all kinds of free gear. And the other thing, the *chicas* were chasing him like wild. You should see some of the emails and messages and even photos they'd send him. Man, I wished so much that was me…"

"You said 'endorsements,' is that right?" Smith interrupted.

"Yeah, all the big companies were after him."

"What did he have to do? I mean was he making videos, or ads, or—"

"Are you kidding? No, not that," Gutiérrez said. "Never his photo, never on video. The only thing anyone ever saw of the famous DC Lovelace was his avatar. It was a blond, muscular kid with kinda long hair, you know the type. I mean if they saw the real thing, the real Don Lovelace, I don't think that would have been the right image. A short, fat kid with thick glasses. A real nerd. But the DC Lovelace everybody saw back then was more of a video character, a superhero who really existed and was one of the best damn gamers that ever was."

The interview went on in the same vein for another ten

minutes or so before the FBI agent asked why Lovelace created a new identity and took his life in a different direction. "Oh, that...," Gutiérrez began. "I can't say exactly, but I remember this conversation about 'nothing being real' in the video world we was living in. And I said he was making good money and was famous and all, and he—Don—said that he didn't want to be some good-looking blond superhero icon avatar, that he wanted to be himself and so he had to create that just like he created the DC Lovelace character, but this time in the real world. So all of a sudden he dropped out, and the next thing you know he's living in an apartment and going to the local college and so on—you know what happened, I guess?"

"Did you keep in touch?" Smith asked.

"Oh, yeah, I mean we was buds, you know. The worst thing was having to remember his new name—Moule. I had trouble pronouncing it even. But he said it was a French word that means 'mussel,' those things like oysters that live in rivers or the ocean. I asked him why he picked that and he said it was like his life, hard on the outside, protected by a shell, but soft and tasty on the inside. Or something *extraño* like that."

For the next few minutes the interview turned to Moule's new character and the multiple years of education that followed. During this time, the two friends drifted apart, having last seen each other just as Moule was starting his PhD program at Stanford. "So when did you reconnect after that?" Smith asked.

"It was after he got into online trading. Don didn't want to work for anyone, so he was independent, kinda...," Gutiérrez began.

"What do you mean by that?" Smith asked.

"He coulda worked for one of those big stock trading companies, but I remember him saying that he didn't want to be a 'cog in somebody else's wheel'—I remember exactly what he said because I didn't know the word 'cog' in English—it's *diente*—'tooth' in Spanish. Anyway he traded stuff online independently." The prisoner paused. "And that's when I got into what ended me up here."

"How so?"

A look of dismay was evident on the enlarged view of Gutiérrez's face. He took a deep breath, then exhaled. "Don was my friend," he finally said. "He made things look so easy that I thought I could do the same thing. I had saved a little money and watched what he did with it—he made a lot more for me. And since he was independent and didn't work for anyone, I thought I could be successful like him. So I started out and was pitching my stuff to the Latino community and got a bunch of folks investing and..." He stopped. "Things didn't go well. So here I am."

"I see," Smith said. "I'd like to hear more about who Moule was doing trading for, if you know."

"I do," Gutiérrez said, "but this has gotta be off the record, okay?"

"Okay," Smith said.

CHAPTER 28

"If we're gonna talk about DC's trading and investing after he got into that business, you need to know what happened before all that, before he changed his name. It's gonna take a while. You okay with that?" Gutiérrez began.

"I've got all day and can come back tomorrow if I need to," Smith said.

"Well, it was like this…," the prisoner began. After high school, most of the members of the Bulldog Gamers club, and others in the small circle of gaming and computer nerds, went on to college or technical school, pursuing careers in information technology, electronics, computer networking and the like. "But see," Gutiérrez said, "DC was a famous gamer. He could afford to move out on his own and live pretty well, and was making more at age eighteen than most of the teachers with their college educations and stuff. So he kept on doing what he was doing. As for me, I just hung around, living at home, working temp jobs and playing video games. We kept in touch with the guys that went off to school. Some of 'em outgrew gaming, and others got more into it, but a lot of 'em were also discovering new political-type things, like the environment and racial justice and all that stuff. Now, you've got to understand that most videogaming is kinda the same as the real world. There are good guys—always our side—and bad guys—the rest of the others—and our goal is to battle them until we win. We might do that by finding our way through a digital maze or collecting online tokens or whatever, but a lot of the games, especially the ones we liked, were shooting games."

"What do you mean by 'shooting games'?" Smith asked.

"Remember I mentioned Warcraft games?"

"Yes."

"In those games, our side—the good guys—are from the Eastern Kingdoms and we battle against the orcs, ugly, mean, kinda human-like beasts who make up the Orcish Horde. So…"

"Whoa," Smith said. "You're losing me there talking about gaming. Just maybe give me a summary."

Gutiérrez frowned and thought for a moment. "Okay. Some, but not many, of our gaming buddies started becoming what they call 'activists' for things they thought were important. Some of them formed groups to—I remember what they called it—'bring about social change.' Only a very few of those groups are still around, but they have gotten into protesting, and demonstrations, and sometimes violence, like after the cop killed that black dude, George Floyd, up in Minnesota." He stopped and looked at Smith, who was scribbling notes. "That good enough?"

"For a start, yeah. I think I see what you're getting at."

"I haven't finished," Gutiérrez said.

"Go ahead. I promise not to say anything more until you do," Smith responded.

"So…and this is from what I kinda learned and figured out, not what DC told me. When he started investing and trading on his own, some of our old gaming friends got in touch with him. Or maybe he called them—I don't know. Anyway, he ended up investing some of their money in cryptocurrencies, and musta done real well, 'cause pretty soon a bunch of those types was asking him to handle money things for them. They liked him 'cause they'd known him since way back, and as a gamer he was or had been one of them. But the most important thing was what he wasn't. He wasn't the government, or the IRS, or one of those nosy people who want to watch what you're doing. It was all secret, more or less, kinda 'off the books,' like I heard one of them say."

"Okay," Smith said, laying down his pen and looking directly at Gutiérrez. "Were any of those groups involved in activities that might attract the government or law enforcement if they knew where to look?"

Gutiérrez's eyes darted rapidly from one side to the other, reflexly looking to see if anyone was watching. "This is all confidential, right?"

"Correct. You're providing valuable information for an ongoing investigation, and you're not sworn. We're looking for leads; we're not after you," Smith replied.

"Then yeah, several of them. I knew that, but DC, he was always kinda out in his own fantasy world, la-la land or somewhere. He was zoned in on making money and didn't care—or didn't ask—what the people did with it."

"Okay," Smith said again. "If I read you a list of names of people and groups, will you tell me if you know or have heard of any of them?"

Again, Gutiérrez's eyes darted about. "Same promises?" Smith nodded.

Extracting several sheets from his briefcase, the agent began slowly reading a list of names of organizations that were known or suspected to have engaged in, or were at risk of engaging in, "domestic terrorism." I had not heard of most of the names and had no idea what they were suspected of doing. Gutiérrez said he was reasonably sure that two of the groups were among those who had at one time or another traded with Moule. Smith then read a list of approximately fifty names of individuals who were on the government's watch list. None of them were familiar.

Smith's attention and questioning then turned to the two groups the prisoner had tentatively identified. The first, the Defenders of Liberty, had worked closely with Moule for a couple of years after he became well established in his trading routine. Gutiérrez didn't know much about them, other than the fact that Moule had mentioned casually to him on more than one occasion that they were "a pain in the ass" and made some unreasonable demands that he could not fulfill. He thought Moule had fired them as clients but wasn't sure. In contrast, he seemed quite familiar with the other group, the American Sojourners. "Oh, yeah, I remember them well. Are they still around? I've been locked up here for a while but I know they were buddies with DC right up until I was arrested."

"They're still active. How did you know them so well?" Smith asked.

"They're all ex-gamers. Guys mostly, with a few women— not many *guapas* though."

"*Guapas?*"

"Sorry, pretty chicks. I don't think those kind of groups attract good-looking women." Gutiérrez paused.

"Do you know anything about the activities of this group, the American Sojourners?"

"A little, yeah."

"If you don't mind my asking, were you ever a member, or how were you involved with them?"

"Oh, I wasn't involved. You see"—Gutiérrez hesitated— "I guess the best way to put it was that I didn't qualify for membership, or being included, or whatever you call it…"

"Why?" Smith seemed puzzled.

"I think the best thing to say is that the group has the name 'American.' In their world, I'm not an 'American' because my parents were from Guatemala and came into the country illegally. I was born in El Paso, so I'm legal, but you know…" His voice tapered off.

"So how did you get familiar with the group?" Smith asked.

"Like I said, there were not many women, but there was one or two who liked guys like me. One of them, Tiffany—I don't remember her last name—called me her 'Latin lover.' We went out for a while and then kinda fell apart. She was a nurse or worked in a hospital or something and then I think she dropped out of the group."

"That's good, but what did the group do?"

"They met pretty regular as I remember. Sometimes Tiff—that's what I called her—would go out of town for protests, to carry signs and that kind of thing. I went with her once, but it was a mistake. They made a big deal of my background so she sent me home. I told Don about it and he said they were assholes, and I shouldn't worry about it." Gutiérrez stared at the table for a moment. "That's about all I know."

"Okay, that's helpful," Smith said. "I want to show you a picture of something and ask you to tell me if you recognize it." Gutiérrez smiled slightly, seeming relieved not to be talking about Tiffany and the American Sojourners. Smith took a sheet of paper out of a folder, held it up briefly before the camera, then placed it on the table in front of the prisoner.

"Oh, the flag of Kek. Yeah, of course," Gutierrez began.

"What do you know about it?" Smith asked.

"It's a gaming thing—or was, anyway. I've been out of touch in here," he said, motioning toward the walls of the prison room. "Like I said, in that world, especially in the Warcraft games, it's us against them. Some gamers sort of said this was our flag, the flag of the good guys. I don't know much about how it got started or where it came from, but it was part of the made-up story you told about your side in that online world. And then some of the people in the activist groups started using it as kind of a sign, or a symbol, or something like that so they could recognize one another. I think you'd say it was like a secret handshake or a secret word you would say to let somebody know you were into the same thing."

"Would a copy of this flag ever have been worn as a tattoo?" Smith interjected.

"Yes, that's what I was just gonna say. Tiff had one on her upper back on the right side. And I guess you know, too, that DC had one?" With this revelation, those of us watching the video gave a spontaneous, simultaneous gasp.

CHAPTER 29

The formerly silent room was suddenly filled with voices saying, "Stop the video," "I need to hear that again," and the like. Hasty did as requested, going back a minute or so and replaying several times Gutiérrez's comment about Moule having the flag tattoo "somewhere on his back."

Briefly flipping on the overhead lights, Hasty said, "That was unexpected, for sure. But we need to finish watching the whole interview to see what else we discover before we start discussing things." The group agreed, and the video of Agent Smith's interview with Arturo Gutiérrez continued for another half hour, failing to produce any significant new disclosures or surprises. At the end, Hasty turned the lights back on and asked in turn for comments and suggestions from each of us. The general consensus seemed to be that Moule was almost certainly doing investments and cryptocurrency trading for shady groups, but seemed naive and probably unaware of the groups' activities. That led to the conjecture that for some reason, he figured things out or decided to stop and perhaps refused to return some funds. That could have been, and probably was, the cause of his death. But the real bombshell was Gutiérrez's statement that Moule possibly had a flag tattoo somewhere on his body.

As the discussion was going on, Labonsky disappeared for a few minutes and returned carrying a bulky expanding file folder. "I have the crime scene report here," he said, tapping the folder, "plus photos and Moule's autopsy report. Give me a minute or two to see what I can find." The table was silent as the detective shuffled through the files. "Okay," he said, "here's the crime scene report and photos, and here's the autopsy report. I'm pretty sure some photos would have been taken as part of that procedure, but they're probably still at the medical examiner's office." He slid the autopsy report, a few thin pages, over to Hasty. "You want to go over this and share it while I sort through this crime scene report?"

Hasty nodded and began reading over the pathologist's dictation. His comments were brief and to the point. "There's nothing specifically in here about a tattoo or other skin marking. There is a notation that photographs were taken, but no direct references to them otherwise." No one said anything. "You know, though," Hasty continued, "tattoos are getting so common these days that it could be the ME didn't see any reason to document them. I think we need to get our hands on the actual photos before we decide Gutiérrez was wrong." Everyone agreed with the suggestion, with Marsh saying he would try to have them for the group by the next morning.

Meanwhile, Labonsky had been going over the crime scene report and flipping through a stack of photos taken at Moule's house on the day of his death. "There's nothing specific in this written report, either," he said. "The description of the body is pretty generic, and there are no special comments on tattoos or similar marks. Of course, we had no way of knowing back then that they might be important. So, the photos…some of them are pretty shocking, but we're all adults here and we're trying to catch a murderer. I'm just going to pass them around. Study them as long as you need to and then give them to the next guy. If you see something on a specific photo, jot it down and we'll talk about it. They're all numbered." With that he slid the pile across the table to the sketch artist, Hartley. The top photo displayed an especially gory full-color view of Moule's exploded cranium. Delicately, Hartley picked up the pile and glanced at the photo, rapidly turning a whiter shade of pale before leaping out of his chair and rushing toward the conference room door, his hand over his mouth. Within seconds of the door shutting, gagging sounds could be heard coming from the hall. "Guess some folks are just not cut out for this type of work," Labonsky observed, a slight smirk on his face.

After a brief discussion of the crime scene photos, Hasty took over once again, glancing at this watch and saying, "I want to thank everyone for being here. It's nearly half past seven and I know we all want to get home. I think we've made some real progress moving this investigation forward. And I want to especially thank John, who came up with the idea of tracking down Moule's high school gaming buddies." Hasty paused, looking at his notes. "We've got a lot of work to do yet. As you all know, this flag tattoo thing got started with the person who calls herself Sarah. It's proving to be the lead we've been hoping for. And I guess it should be obvious to everyone that the person Gutierrez called 'Tiffany' and the suspect 'Sarah' may be the same person. As soon as we leave here, I'm going to start making some calls to follow up on that possibility. And the other thing we need…"

"…is to follow up on the autopsy photos," Labonsky said, finishing Hasty's sentence for him. A brief moment of silence followed as the two men locked eyes. "I apologize for elbowing in there, Jim, but sometimes I think I need to remind you that I'm still the lead detective on this case, and you're a liaison from the FBI."

Hasty smiled slightly, clenching his jaw muscles in the process. "Point well taken, Rod. I apologize. Do you want to take over?"

"No," Labonsky said, "but let's meet in this room tomorrow afternoon at two o'clock. Jim, it would be helpful if you could have something from the Bureau by then on this American Sojourners group. And John, you need to be here; you've seen more of Sarah than anyone else." Catching the reference to the photo of Sarah naked next to me on the bed, a few sneaky smiles appeared on several faces around the room.

I emerged from police headquarters into the late afternoon heat, walking the few blocks back to the gallery and my apartment. The sun was low in the western sky, casting a reddish light on the tops of the live oaks and palm trees along the edge of the old colonial cemetery. I thought about Sarah. I hadn't seen this Tiffany woman Gutierrez spoke of, but there was no way they could be the same person. Of course, if Sarah and Moule and Tiffany all had the same tattoo, and in the same location, there had to be some connection. Maybe they were or had been members of the same group—the American Sojourners or some other one. Or maybe the tattoo was just a tattoo and had little meaning other than a decorative design. I figured we would find out eventually.

At two the next day, the group—minus the sketch artist this time—reassembled to see what Hasty and Labonsky had come up with overnight. Hasty, either angry or cowed by the detective's sniping the evening before, said little and sat quietly while Labonsky took charge once again.

"Okay," he began. "Pete picked up Moule's autopsy photos from the ME's office earlier this morning. Turns out they're interesting, to say the least. You all saw the crime scene photos yesterday. There was lots of blood, as you know. Moule's body was found sitting mostly upright at the head of his bed. The weapon that killed him was placed in his mouth and discharged so that the bullet exited through the upper rear of his scalp, causing significant blood flow over his shoulders and upper back. The medical examiner's techs routinely photographed the body, and the ME himself and the techs both went over it 'in detail,' or so they said. But it seems that below the dried bloodstains on Moule's right upper back there was something they missed. Even though he's been dead for months, his body is unclaimed and still in cold storage in the morgue. So they went back and this time turned the body over and scrubbed off some of the dried blood from the area of interest, just over the"—Labonsky looked at a sheet of paper he was holding—"'spinous process of the right scapula,' according to this auxiliary report issued just this morning. Once the blood was cleaned up, they could see this." He handed out color photos of what appeared to be a tattoo of the same green, black, and white flag partially seen on Sarah's upper back. The skin image appeared old and faded, but how much of that had to do with the condition of the corpse was uncertain.

"So," Labonsky pronounced, "we finally have a link between this flag tattoo, the victim Moule, our prime suspect Sarah, and a group named the American Sojourners." He stopped and surveyed the small group. No one said anything. "Now we have to determine what all this means." Turning to Hasty, he said, "Jim, I believe you have something to say as well."

"I wish I could report a connection, too," Hasty said, "but I can't. I made some calls last night and got the guys back at the Bureau working on it. As I guess you can imagine, this Sojourner group is already on our radar, and without violating any laws, we've been keeping tabs on their activities, which at times has included photographing participants in demonstrations that have turned violent. A former member of the group is named Tiffany Johns, and it just so happens that she was arrested for trespassing with several other Sojourners about three years ago. We got a copy of her mug shot and sent it to the warden at the Beaumont prison, who in turn showed it to

Señor Gutierrez. He identified her as his former girlfriend. Subsequently, she has gotten married, settled down, and lives in the Dallas area. She's now the mother of a set of nine-month-old twins. I don't believe she's our girl."

For some strange reason, I felt relieved.

CHAPTER 30

Back home that evening in the silence of my apartment, I spent a long time staring at the wall and thinking about what, if anything, I should do next. This whole affair, which had taken over my life now for months, was not of my making. I figured that if I could escape without any personal damage, I shouldn't be worried about the outcome. Or such was my reasoning. I had nothing to do with Moule's death or whatever groups of baddies he might have gotten tangled up with. I had to admit that the lure of money got me involved in the first place, but nothing had come of that. Whatever might happen from here on out, it should be no concern of mine.

On the other hand, I had become involved in the investigation, almost as a member of the team. I'd had a close encounter with Sarah, one of the leading suspects in Moule's murder. Someone had tried to kill me because they erroneously assumed—by default—that I had knowledge of what happened to something of great value, presumably money or its digital equivalent. One group—Sarah's—said it was theirs and wanted it back. The other group—which lost two members in the car crash—didn't want Sarah or anyone else to get their hands on it. I had assisted in making some significant contributions to the investigation, yet it seemed bogged down in part because of conflict between Hasty, representing the feds, and Labonsky, representing the local cops. I just wanted it all to end. I just wanted my life back, however dull or challenging or exciting it might be. I reached the conclusion that someone needed to make a brave move to push the inquiry toward its resolution. It seemed that someone needed to be me. Tossing the known facts and options back and forth in my mind, I set out to devise a plan.

Based on my understanding of all that had happened, Sarah held the key to unlocking many of the unknowns in the investigation. She was most likely the female seen at Moule's house on the day of his murder. Both she and Moule evidently had the same unique tattoo. Assuming she was the one, she obviously knew the identity of the man who accompanied her there and the details of Moule's death. She knew the general nature of Moule's investments and the name of the "other" opposing group for which he was working. She apparently knew the names of the two guys killed in the wreck. There were abundant reasons to justify her arrest, yet it seemed that both Hasty and Labonsky were not being especially aggressive in pursuing that option. Technically, Labonsky was in charge, so he should be the one pushing in that direction. But it could be that the feds did not want her arrested at this point, as it might upset some ongoing domestic terrorism probe. Maybe the timing of her eventual arrest was less important than I imagined; a charge of murder has no statute of limitations. If or when the Savannah cops got custody of her, the ability to prosecute her for Moule's murder, either directly or as an accessory, would not be an issue.

I knew I would be a total fool if I believed the investigators had not thoroughly discussed all these thoughts and questions. For whatever reason, however, they had not shared their overall plan with me, and thus my ordeal dragged on. I needed to do something about that. The one thing I had going for my plan was Sarah's continuing attempt to recover whatever she thought I had gotten from Moule. She had promised to call me, and that could lead to a meeting between us. I didn't think she—or anyone working with her—would try to harm me at this point if they believed I held the key to Moule's missing funds. If they got rid of me, they'd never see their money or whatever else they were after.

The challenge now was how to implement my vague idea, making it work for the investigators and bringing an end to the investigation—at least the part that involved me. Maybe then I could take a deep breath and get on with my life. I couldn't go it alone, taking things into my own hands. I had to let someone know what I was doing. Holloway was out of the picture at this point, and that meant choosing between Hasty, whom I personally liked and respected, and Labonsky, whom I was less fond of but who had been upfront, honest, and helpful to me thus far. It was one or the other, I reasoned. If I presented it to both of them, I feared they'd squabble over the details and end up nixing the whole idea. I didn't discount Pete Marsh, of course, but he wasn't in charge and would take Labonsky's side, I was sure. Sitting at my kitchen table, I grabbed a legal pad and began to sketch out the plan I wanted to present. An hour and several revisions later, I had it. I relaxed, fixed myself a cup of herbal tea, and went to bed for the night.

I called Labonsky the next morning, telling him I wanted to discuss the case privately with him. He agreed to meet me at my apartment at noon and not mention our meeting to anyone. Sitting on my couch, with me opposite in a comfortable chair, he said, "Okay, John, tell me what's up."

"As you may have figured out," I began, "I've been really frustrated with the slow pace of this Moule investigation. It's eating into my life and basically everything I do—or want to do. I want to get off this merry-go-round. You know as well as I do that the only way for that to happen is to wrap the whole thing up."

"True," Labonsky said, his tone noncommittal.

"So, I want to present a plan to accomplish that. It

involves Sarah, and what I hope will be her arrest at some point soon. You know she called me again the other day?"

"Yeah, Pete Marsh told me," Labonsky said, sitting up and leaning forward, listening more intently now.

"She and whoever she's working with are convinced I know where or how to get whatever Moule was holding for them—money or its equivalent, I assume. I lied to her and told her I did, but said I'd consider finding a way for her to recover it for a price, a small commission…"

"Were you lying to her, John?" Labonsky said. "There's always been a question in our minds."

"Yes," I replied, but wasn't sure he believed me. "I want to arrange a meeting with Sarah. She said she would call me back after she talked with some of her people. I don't want to wear a wire or have a bunch of undercover cops hanging around. I've thought about it, and I'm certain they won't try to harm me, especially since she thinks I know how to recover what she wants. I'll see if I can't get her to answer questions we have, like what was Moule's relationship to these groups, the Sojourners and the Bunker Hill people. And other questions, too. We can go over all that before I meet with her. Then, after we've talked, she goes back to wherever she came from. No arrest until we agree to meet again for me to turn over information on how to get what she wants. Then she's off the street and I have nothing else to do with any of this."

"You know you'd probably have to testify at a trial—or trials," Labonsky said.

"I can do that."

Labonsky was silent for a long moment, obviously digesting my proposal. "I don't know if you've realized it, but I've been pushing to get this Sarah person arrested since she first popped up. But Hasty and the feds have other ideas. They want to work on this from the other end, look at the big picture first and scoop up the players when they've figured it all out. And that's about all they'll share with me—some national security bullshit reason."

"That's the other thing," I said. "I don't want anyone but you to know about this plan, what I want to do. Assuming it works, you can say Sarah insisted on meeting with me and take credit for her arrest."

"So, let me be sure I've got this straight. This plan you've worked up is just between me and you and, I guess, Sarah, right?"

"That's what I'm suggesting," I said. "I don't mean to screw up whatever the FBI has going on, but I've had about all I can take. I think I'm being used."

"Okay," Labonsky said. "I need to think about this overnight. Moule's murder is one facet of something larger—that's why the feds are involved. And I want to say upfront that I don't want to get myself in a situation where it looks like I went rogue to help wrap up an investigation that was tangled in other people's priorities. Is that clear? Can we agree on that before we say or do anything else? I need deniability, and there may be times you'll have to cover for me."

"I'll do that," I said, "but I expect you to do the same for me. We both have the same goal, getting this investigation wrapped up." Labonsky reached out and shook my hand.

I ate a light lunch, feeling encouraged, then spent the remainder of the afternoon at the gallery, catching up on the things I had put off in favor of worrying about the Moule case. I had said it before, but now I was sure. The end of this nightmare was in sight.

As if on cue, Sarah called just before six. The gallery had closed for the day and I was back in my apartment, reading the

Savannah newspaper online. Again, the screen message on my phone read "Unknown Caller." I answered with "Hello, Sarah."

"John, you knew it was me. How lovely." She paused, then, "How are you?"

"I'm fine, and you?" I replied, phatic speech as the linguists would say, designed to set the tone and gauge the mood of the impending conversation.

"I'm actually doing well. I discussed your proposal with the others, and they will agree to some form of reward, or reimbursement for your troubles, or whatever you want to call it." She sounded positive.

"That's good to hear. What are we talking about, approximately at least?" I asked, wanting to appear greedy.

"Assuming we recover all that is due us, and assuming that the value of the assets has not changed, we would offer roughly $500,000. That's half a million dollars, John. A lot of money."

"It is," I said. "And it sounds reasonable, all considered. But we need to meet, to talk about some things, to work out the details. Also, I have some questions I want answered before I return anything."

"John, John…," Sarah said, pausing. "You know we both have our secrets. I don't want mine exposed any more than you would if, say, the police were to find out you made off with Moule's digital wallet. That alone would make you an accessory and likely land you in prison." Sarah used the term "digital wallet." I wasn't sure what she was referring to, but I couldn't let her know.

"You're right. We both need to keep our secrets. But let's at least meet and discuss things."

"For sure. But you've been cooperating with the police. We can't have any of that, you realize. If you show up wearing

175

a wire, or with undercover cops lurking around and waiting to arrest me, bad things will happen to you as well."

"I realize that. So where do you propose we meet?" I asked.

"Well, I've been thinking about that. How about at the top of the lighthouse on Tybee Island one morning just after it opens and before the crowds appear?'"

"Okay," I said. "How will I…?"

Without allowing me to finish my question Sarah said, "I'll call you with the details." The line went dead.

CHAPTER 31

Two days passed with no word from Sarah. I realized that if I wanted to convince her that I knew how to access Moule's funds, I couldn't appear as totally naïve as I actually was. I vaguely recalled him mentioning something that sounded like "cryptowallets" the first time I visited his house when he attempted—without much success—to give me a quick education on cryptocurrencies and how they differed from the usual stock and security trading. I settled down in front of my laptop and set out to educate myself—not as an expert, but enough to make Sarah think I understood what I had supposedly received from Moule.

After several hours of reading and rereading, I felt I had a basic understanding of the system. The most important concept, or so it seemed to me, was what Moule had kept repeating: "It's not real." Cryptocurrencies, like many other things humans hold near and dear, don't really exist, at least in physical form. We talk about love, or patriotism, or religion, but they're concepts that we more or less agree on, with different meanings to different people. Cryptocurrency exists only in digital form, positive and negative charges marking zeros and ones inside a myriad of computer servers, but with the understanding that they can be converted to dollars—or euros, or yen, or pounds sterling, or any of a dozen other currencies that can be spent in countries around the world. The fundamental advantage of cryptocurrency is that the record of its existence is filed in "blockchains," shared databases on multiple interlinked computer servers. No single entity, such as a government agency or international bank or some private company like Google, oversees the network. The databases are designed to be permanent and publicly available, but the owners of the cryptocurrency in them are identified only by codes. The cryptocurrency account itself holds credits for any of multiple individual types of cryptocoins with names such as Bitcoin, Dogecoin, Ethereum, and others. The only person who can make changes to an account is the holder of a complex digital key—a long string of numbers and letters. This, I discovered, is held in a "digital wallet." That—apparently a file on a flash drive or other storage medium—seemed to be what everyone was searching for. Given the anonymity and what appeared to be the ease of recovering the funds once the digital key was in hand, anyone—Sarah's group, "the others" as she called them, even me—could secretly become very wealthy with a few clicks on a keyboard. Not the absolute perfect crime for every thief, but it came close.

Taking a break from my studying, I called Labonsky to give him the details of our earlier conversation and Sarah's suggestion that we meet at the Tybee lighthouse. "Not a bad choice for her," he observed. "It's pretty much open ground there. It'd be hard for a bunch of undercover cops to blend into a crowd, especially early in the morning before the tourists get there." We decided to meet at my apartment after work to go over things, in particular what I was planning to do or say if, as he put it, "she doesn't change her mind and actually shows up." Labonsky seemed somewhat doubtful that she would follow through.

The detective knocked on my door just after seven o'clock. "Sorry I'm late," he apologized. "I worked through lunch and was kinda hungry. Had to stop at the deli and get a bite to eat." He neglected mentioning the obvious: since his wife left him there was no one to go home to, no one to share dinner with. I explained to him that I wanted to meet twice with Sarah. The first time, which I presumed would be at Tybee, would be to negotiate the terms of my supposedly turning over the key to Moule's money. In fact, I wanted to use that meeting to find out as much as possible about what went on the day of his murder and what led him to transfer his accounts overseas beyond anyone's reach. Labonsky had previously suggested there was still a lingering suspicion that I might have some involvement—not in the murder but in making off with knowledge of the missing funds. And, more out of curiosity than anything else, I wanted to know about why someone from the Bunker Hill Militia would try to kill me, if in fact that was what they wanted to do.

"You know damned well she's not going to tell you all that," Labonsky said. "You gotta explain your curiosity, and if I were her, I'd think you were working for the cops." He snorted. "In the crime business, the less said the better."

"Of course, but I can be truthful about that and tell her I'm just curious. Why did all this get dumped on me? Just what made everyone think I'd made off with Moule's money? This has made my life miserable lately, not to mention nearly getting me killed." I found myself a little angry at Labonsky's attitude. "I'm presenting this to Sarah as a *quid pro quo*," I continued. "I give them the way to retrieve their money, and she shares information with me." Labonsky didn't respond. "And, of course, I'll be lying to her. I have no idea where Moule's money is or how to get it back."

"Hmmm," Labonsky said. "I thought there was supposed to be honor even among thieves," his voice tinged with sarcasm. After a few seconds he asked, "And what is this *quid pro quo* thing?"

We talked for another half hour. He said if, or when, Sarah called back and set up a time to meet, he would be nearby, though not exactly sure where. "I've got to go over to the light-house to get a better feel for the lay of the land. It'll be just me there to back you up, you know that."

"I do," I said.

"And if things go bad, there's just so much I can do without a crew."

"I'm willing to risk that."

"It's your ass," Labonsky said, almost dismissively.

"I can handle it," I said.

"And that's the first of two meetings you're planning, right? And the second time, when you're supposed to turn over the keys to Moule's fortune, when is that gonna happen, and what are your plans when it does?" Labonsky continued.

"Pretty simple. You and Hasty swoop in and arrest her."

"Why not arrest her after your first meeting? You get the info you want, then flash us a signal and in we come?"

"That was my first thought, but there are too many loose ends, too many things we don't know. Think about it. There were two people on the video of Moule's house on the day he was killed. Who was the guy? And was it the same guy who planted a camera at my apartment? Somebody was behind try-ing to kill me by causing me to wreck—who were those people and what was their motive? What was Moule's relationship to these 'activist' groups whose money he was supposed to invest? If you just hone in on Sarah and arrest her, everyone else goes underground. I know you and Jim Hasty have your disagree-ments, but Moule's murder appears to be one of several crimes that involve a whole group of people. Sarah is just one of them."

Labonsky's eyes narrowed as I spoke. "You're beginning to sound like Hasty, John. I'm a homicide cop in charge of a murder investigation, and you're talking about letting the one who did it walk out under our very noses. What if she catches on, or panics and splits? Where does that put us then—back at square one, maybe? Yeah, the feds make a point with their 'domestic terrorism' talk, but do you let a potential murder suspect walk free just for the sake of the investigation? I don't like it."

"But will you help me? Will you back me up?"

"Yeah, but it's not my first choice of the way to handle this," Labonsky said, frowning. "All I can do is hope and pray that your plan doesn't blow up in our faces. That wouldn't be good for either one of us."

CHAPTER 32

Now I had to wait for Sarah's call, and in my usual compulsive way paraded the options and scenarios through my mind. She wasn't in charge; that seemed clear. She needed to consult with others before making decisions. At the same time, I had no idea who these people were. Other committed members of the American Sojourners, or some other group? And what would they do once Labonsky took Sarah into custody? Would that put a huge target on my back, especially since they might believe I still held the key to unlock Moule's digital treasure chest?

What had made them so sure I had it in the first place? That seemed to be a fundamental question I had failed to ask. I thought about what I knew of the timeline on the day of Moule's death. I had an appointment with him that afternoon at 2:00 p.m. Sarah and an unknown man showed up at his house at 9:30, about four and a half hours before I was set to arrive. They stayed two and a half, maybe three hours and then left. Working the crime scene later, the police techs noted that some flash drives and non-connected storage devices, the sort of places where one would keep a secret digital key, were missing. Why did everyone think I had taken them, or even that Moule had given the key to me? Maybe Sarah would tell me and, more importantly, explain why Moule was murdered.

The call came late the next afternoon. "Hi, John," Sarah said, her voice as silky as before. "Do you still want to meet with me tomorrow morning?"

"I do," I said, my heart hammering, "but only to get acquainted and have some questions answered. If I give you the key, I'll be joining the criminal conspiracy…"

"Oh, John, stop being a lawyer. You're just helping us

182

recover what is ours."

I didn't let her finish. "Something you murdered a man for."

"Moule's death was an accident," Sarah said. "He had been one of us. It shouldn't have happened."

"So someone putting a gun in his mouth and blowing the back of his head off was an accident? You'd have a hard time convincing a jury of that, Sarah."

She was silent for a moment, then said, "Why don't we talk about it tomorrow? There's no sense arguing this out on the phone now. I...I got a call last night from someone. Someone who knows what's going on. John, we have to be so very, very careful in what we do or say." I heard anxiety in her voice.

"Okay," I said, and waited for her response.

"Here's what I want you to do. The Tybee lighthouse opens to visitors at 9:00 a.m. I'll be there when it does; you get there about five minutes later so we don't buy our tickets or walk in together. I'll meet you at the base of the lighthouse— I'll be sitting on a bench. I want you to wear a polo shirt and shorts, no socks."

"Why the hell...?"

"I want to make sure you're not wearing a wire," Sarah responded.

"I'm not that crazy."

"Don't you think we're crazy to be doing all this in the first place?" she asked. "I'll be by myself, but I'll have help nearby if I need it."

"Anything else?" I asked.

"Just show up tomorrow morning. If there is any sign at all of undercover cops hanging out, I'll leave. I want to be sure you understand that." Sarah's voice was firm now.

"I do."

"Then I'll see you a little after nine tomorrow morning." Again, the line went dead with a click.

I called Labonsky and went over the details of the conversation. "So she wants you to dress down, eh? Polo shirt and shorts? That's a hoot. But a smart way to check for wires and bugs. Reckon she'll want you to drop trou once you get in the privacy of the lighthouse?"

"I have no idea, but I think she's already seen me mostly naked. At this point I really don't care."

"Okay, let's do it. I'll be there tomorrow, but as a tourist. And I'll keep my distance from you two." He paused. "Unless something happens."

At 9:05 a.m. the next morning, I pulled into the near-empty parking lot of the Tybee Light Station, located on the northeast corner of Tybee Island about fifteen miles east of downtown Savannah. It was a place where I had spent many wonderful days of my childhood during the several years I lived with my grandparents. The pleasant memories had now turned to fear and apprehension as I parked and purchased my entry ticket. "Out early this morning?" the lady in the ticket kiosk said, smiling. I smiled back and nodded without replying. The lighthouse itself rises nearly 150 feet above the surrounding buildings, formerly home to keepers of the light but now a museum and administrative offices. Tybee lighthouse, like most such structures, ceased to be of major navigational importance with the introduction of wireless and later satellite-based location systems. It's now maintained as a tourist attraction and historical monument.

I entered the grounds, glancing about for Sarah. To my left, an elderly couple walked hand in hand toward the museum. To my right, at the base of the tower, a blonde woman in a summer dress studied a brochure displaying historical images of the lighthouse. She looked up and, with a subtle flash of recognition, disappeared into the tower stairway. So Sarah had changed her hair color back to blonde. Trying to appear casual, I ambled over to the tower entrance, past a small office and historical display and into the circular stairwell with its 178 steps leading to the light far above.

Being the first visitors of the day, we had the tower to ourselves. Sarah's footsteps echoed off the walls as she trudged up the steps above me. At first she was out of sight, but with a small burst of speed I closed the gap between us until she was only yards ahead me. I could hear each of her soft footfalls on the cast-iron treads and her slightly labored breathing as she tried to maintain a constant pace to the top. Her progress slowed slightly, closing the gap between us as the diameter of the tapering tower narrowed. By the time we reached the light room just below the massive Fresnel lens, I could have reached out and touched the hem of her dress if I chose to do so. Exhausted and too winded to speak, we both leaned against the walls as our breathing and heart rate slowed. Between deep breaths I said, "You changed your hair color."

"I'm a natural blonde," Sarah said, still gasping.

"I know," I said, leading her to burst into laughter as best she could.

"That was a stupid thing for me to say," she said. "But first things first, John. Come here." She extracted a small instrument from a fanny pack and waved it over my shirt and shorts. It squealed as it passed my watch.

"What's that?" I asked.

"A little device that lets me know if you're wearing a radio transmitter or anything metallic. I want to be sure that whatever we say remains private." She glanced at a meter on the device, turned it off and stuffed it back in the small pack, saying, "You're clean."

Another minute passed as we tried to recover from the climb. Sarah's eyes swept around the small room, fixing for a moment on a video camera mounted overhead. "Why don't we go out on the gallery? It's more private." She pushed open a small door leading to the narrow porch that circled the top of the lighthouse. The beacon, now dark during daylight hours, loomed over us inside its glass-enclosed space. The clear sky was a perfect shade of blue as a mild seaward breeze cooled the morning heat. To the east, the Atlantic Ocean disappeared into the horizon, and I thought I could just make out the southern tip of Hilton Head Island in South Carolina to the north. We were all alone, just Sarah and me. What a strange place, I thought, to talk about murder and larceny and lies and deception.

"You said you had some questions you wanted answered," Sarah said, breaking my reverie. "Ask me."

"Tell me about Moule," I said. "Everything."

CHAPTER 33

"I almost don't know where to start," Sarah began. "This whole thing has been a nightmare, something that began innocently enough, got bigger and bigger, and then blew up. There's so much and it's so complicated..."

"I'm in no rush. Why don't you start at the beginning?" I said.

Sarah glanced at her watch. "I don't want to stay here too long. I'll try to hit the highlights first, but you need to know everything." She took a deep breath and began. "I was a bit of a geek in high school when I first got into computers and gaming, and for a few years there it kinda took over my life. I was especially into the Warcraft games, and one of my heroes, the person that everyone wanted to be, was this guy, DC Lovelace. He was some mysterious person—in fact, all we ever saw of him was his avatar, a handsome digital dude who was probably one of the best gamers that ever existed. I mean, his endorsement of just about anything from cereal to soft drinks would make us want to buy it. He was big. And then one day the ads and promotions featuring him just disappeared, and those of us who followed him—especially the girls—figured the ad agencies had just moved on to something else. Like I said, though, no one had ever seen him in the flesh, and some people began to think DC Lovelace never really existed, that he was a character who had just been created by some ad agency like Captain Morgan, the rum pirate, or the Dos Equis guy in those beer commercials. But I'd seen him in action online in gaming sites and chat rooms and knew he was a real person.

"So then there was college. I went to Pitzer College in California. One of the things they push there is social activism, a

187

lot of which is basically anti-American. I mean, I grew up in south Georgia, and all this crap about how America is basically a racist country dominated by rich white men and how the only thing George Washington should be remembered for is the fact that he was a slave owner just turned me off. I ended up joining a small group of campus patriots, a number of which turned out to have been into video games. Because we didn't suck up to whatever socialist bullshit the college was putting out, we became social exiles and ended up making our meetings secret. After graduation, I moved back to Georgia and got my MBA from Georgia State in Atlanta. But two of the guys in our college group went on to do social activism full time. One organized the American Sojourners—I'm a member of that group—and the other the Bunker Hill Militia, which pushes the limit between protesting and rioting and maybe even crosses the line into some iffy things legally.

"Okay, so it turns out that we were talking one day, and the subject of gaming came up, and one of the guys in our group said he actually knew DC Lovelace back when, and had kept in touch with him. He said DC had given up the gaming world and gotten a PhD and was doing private investing now, and maybe we should talk with him. But the guy said I was going to be shocked when I met the real man behind the Lovelace avatar. I'll spare you all the details, but we met with Lovelace, who had changed his name to Don Moule. He agreed to help us with our investments. See, we're funded mainly by contributions from people who believe in America, and sometimes the gifts can be quite large, even fifty thousand dollars or more. This was about three years ago, and at the time Don was living in Albuquerque. He said he was looking for a change and decided to move to Savannah. It worked for everyone and—"

"What did you think of Moule when you first met him?"

I interrupted. "I mean, he wasn't exactly the blond, macho avatar known as DC Lovelace."

"Kind of a shock, to be honest. But as I got to know him he turned out to be kind and gentle and probably the smartest person I've ever known, at least with numbers and investing." She hesitated a moment. "But he was kind of naïve, though."

"How do you mean?"

"Well, he was doing really well for our group—great returns and growth of the money we'd given him to invest, a lot of which he put in cryptocurrencies. And we told our friends, so the word got out. Pretty soon Don got the reputation of being the go-to investment guy for activist groups. He never asked a word about their political philosophies or what they actually did, he just invested and got great returns—again mostly in crypto, off the books and away from government spying.

"It appears, though, that someone told him his investments were helping people who advocated violence, so he dumped several big clients and made some people mad in the process. I don't know, but I suspect the person who alerted him was the FBI or Homeland Security maybe. Toward the end, it looks like he was just doing trading for the people he already knew, my group and the Bunker Hill people. But you have to understand that besides that, Don had amassed a small fortune of his own. When things were good, we'd visit sometimes and he would talk about it. I don't know his background, about his family and all of that, but I do know he was proud of his success."

We were standing on the gallery shielded from the steadily rising sun by the lighthouse tower. In the parking lot below, a minivan disgorged a small crowd of kids who, once inside the station, were herded toward the lighthouse entrance by their

189

chaperone. Sarah paused and said, "Looks like we're about to have company. Why don't we go sit in the shade of one of the buildings down below. I think we'll be okay there." I agreed and followed her down the circular stairway, an easier trip in that direction. We found a quiet bench and settled in to finish our conversation.

"None of what you've told me gives any hint on why Moule was killed," I said.

"I know, and I'm getting to that," Sarah responded. "I just want you to understand how things played out." She resumed her account. "Anyway, all was well until two days before the end. That was a Thursday. Don got an unannounced visit from someone—he would never say who, but again I think it was the same people that had warned him earlier, probably the FBI. I have no idea what was said, but the next day he transferred all of his accounts offshore, every single one of them. He still had access, but they were totally out of reach of everyone else. Late that afternoon—it was a Friday—I just happened to check the Sojourner accounts online and discovered they had been drained. I called Billy Jackson—he helps with accounting for the Bunker Hill crowd—and he discovered the same thing. So we called Moule. He said he had moved them to keep them 'safe,' but wouldn't say any more. He agreed to meet us Saturday morning to explain things. Billy and I wanted to find out what was going on before we told the others.

"Well, we got there, and the conversation started off pleasant enough. Then Moule said he'd been warned about doing business with us and that his accounts might get blocked, so he'd moved them out of reach and so on. And Billy got mad, really mad. He threatened to beat Moule up unless he immediately returned the money to us. At that point Billy was standing over him yelling, and Moule was sinking down in his chair and it looked there was about to be a fight, so I jumped in and yelled for Billy to back off, and he did, kinda." Sarah was agitated now as she recounted the events of that morning. "I said let's talk about this like adults. I asked if Moule had some coffee or a bottle of water or something to get him out of the room. He said he did in the fridge, but as he got up to get it, Billy said 'Sit back down!' and stormed out of the room headed toward the kitchen.

"I tried to calm Don, who was drawn up trembling in his chair by this point. About five minutes or so later, Billy comes back in with a tray and three glasses of orange juice. He said he couldn't find any bottled water. Billy was acting calmly now and apologized for his outburst. He handed each of us a glass, and we sat there and tried to talk about things calmly for just a few minutes. And then Moule began to slur his speech and appeared to be drowsing off in the middle of a sentence. I looked at Billy and asked him what the hell was going on, and he said, 'That's what I want to find out, so I put a little surprise in his drink.' And by that time Moule had slumped over and was snoring."

"This is beginning to sound familiar," I said.

"Yeah, unfortunately," Sarah said. I thought I was reading sorrow over the anxiety in her voice. "But just after that is when Moule said he'd given you the key…"

CHAPTER 34

"Why are you telling me all this, Sarah?"

In the span of only a few minutes she had essentially confessed to being present at—if not a participant in—a vicious murder, not to mention a long list of other crimes that would keep a grand jury busy for hours issuing indictments and assure her a lengthy prison term. The lovely, intelligent, and articulate blonde sitting next to me on the bench was either a sociopathic fool or had somehow become involved in events that had spun out of control and drawn her down in the process. "I don't even know your full name," I added, "just Sarah."

"I know and I'm sorry—I'm sorry now for almost everything I've done since I first met you that day in the gallery. Believe me, please, I wasn't doing it for me, but to help support the cause of freedom in this country—that's what the Sojourners stand for. But now I realize I've been an idiot, getting tied up in all this."

"But your name…?"

"It's Sarah. I didn't lie about that. Sarah McKinsey Scott. McKinsey's my maiden name. The part about being divorced is true—no kids."

"Answer my question, please. Why are you telling me all this now?" I demanded.

Sarah looked at me a moment and said, "Because someone else has to know. I have suddenly realized I'm all alone in this…this situation. John, I think I've been used…"

I watched Sarah carefully as she spoke. Was I hearing fear in her voice, or simply the words of an actress playing a part designed to manipulate me like she had before? I didn't know. "Tell me more, then," I said, trying to remain expressionless.

"Why do you want 'someone else' to know, especially me?"

"Because you've become a victim, too. An innocent one for sure, but still a victim."

"Keep talking then. Explain things to me," I said.

"I almost don't know where to start. Billy Jackson was my friend, and sometimes my lover," she began. "And he was the other man who was killed in the car that tried to run you off the road. As far as I know, the investigators haven't figured that out yet. I was living in Atlanta until two years ago when I got divorced. It was ugly, and I thought the best thing to do was start over, so I moved here, to Savannah. I got a good settlement in the divorce; I was going to take my time in finding another job. When I lived in Atlanta, I was active in the local chapter of the Sojourners, and joined the Savannah one shortly after moving here, in part to meet people and maybe have some social life. That's where I met Billy. He was a member of the Bunker Hill group, but we all kind of ran in the same circles. He was their treasurer. Billy was a great guy—trained as an operating room nurse and mainly did short-term job contracts around the Southeast working in hospitals on a temp basis. We had some good times, and both did volunteer stuff for patriot causes. One thing led to another...you know how it is?" Sarah dabbed at her eyes. "The really weird thing, though, was that we'd both been gamers, were both fans of DC Lovelace, and both had the same tattoo."

"You mean the Kekistan flag on your back?"

Sarah gave me a look of shocked surprise. "How did you know...? Oh, yeah, that crazy photo I sent you." I nodded without speaking. "I got that when I was about eighteen because, well, the DC Lovelace gamer avatar had one. And Billy got his about the same time for the same reason. We figured out that it was a sign that we should be together. So we were, but with limits. More close friends with benefits, you know?"

"I do," I said, thinking of Jenna.

"Anyway," she continued, "Billy had slipped some fentanyl in Moule's orange juice. It's a drug they use for sedation in the operating room, and he'd managed to steal some. Too much can be fatal he told me, but a smaller dose can act like a truth serum. People are groggy but will usually answer questions and then have no memory of it when they wake up later. I had never heard of it until that day, and didn't realize what Billy was up to. He said he'd brought some in case Moule 'wouldn't talk.' So we roused him enough to get him to the elevator and up to his bedroom. We knew he had sent our account overseas and wanted to know how to get access. Billy propped Moule up on the bed and started questioning him. About the only useful thing he said was 'I gave the code to John O'Toole. He knows what I want,' or something like that. He repeated it several times. Then the drug apparently started to wear off a little, and Moule got real agitated. Billy slapped him. I told him to stop, but he said he was going to do what it took to 'get our money back.' And then, he reached under his shirt and pulled out a pistol and told Moule he was going to kill him unless he got a straight answer—and at that point I left and went back downstairs. I couldn't take it. There was some yelling and about ten minutes later a gunshot, then everything went quiet. I ran back up the stairs and Billy was standing over Moule and there was blood everywhere and…" Sarah buried her face in her hands and began to sob. All I could do was stare and wonder how she could be such a moron.

I remained silent. Wiping the tears from her eyes, she resumed her story. "Billy said it was an accident. He said he had the gun in Moule's mouth, threatening to pull the trigger, when Moule swatted at his hand and the gun went off. Billy must have been close—he had splashes of blood on his shirt. I screamed when I saw what happened, and I think he kinda panicked then and said, 'We've got to do something. Make this look like an accident or a robbery or a suicide.' And he paced back and forth and then got real calm and said we're going to make it look like he killed himself. And that's when he laid the gun in Moule's hand and kinda straightened things up. He wanted to—"

"Did you search the house?" I interrupted.

"Kinda. Billy's good with...I'm sorry, Billy *was* good with computers and stuff like that, so he found the security system and erased the video recordings. And we both searched Moule's office and grabbed any flash drives or SSDs or the like laying around and took them with us. Turned out they didn't have anything useful on them. And that's when he began to think about what Moule said about giving 'the code' or something to you." She stopped and looked at me a moment. "I'm so sorry, John. I'd be lying if I said *he* just focused on you. We *both* did. I was part of the whole thing. His anger spread to me, and the more he talked about how we'd been 'robbed' the madder I got. I just went along with it. We planned it, the whole thing. I'd find a way to get you alone, we'd drug you like Moule and get you to talk. But I made Billy promise not to bring a gun and not to harm you otherwise. And I guess you know what happened after that. I played the attractive divorcée, and you..."

"I know the rest of the story; you don't have to go into detail," I said. "So did I say anything after you drugged me?"

"No, nothing at all really. You kept asking for Jenna, who I found out later is your girlfriend."

"Why the photo?"

"Possible blackmail. After you passed out, Billy and I were

there alone, and there was the other bedroom and well…. Anyway, we were laying there in bed and he said why don't you pose with O'Toole so we can threaten to show the photo around if he doesn't give us what we want. And I did, but covered up my face. I guess the tattoo gave me away, eh?"

"Billy took the photo?"

"Yeah, I think it kinda turned him on—but let's not talk about that." Sarah was silent after that, staring down at her hands. I wondered if she was thinking about her friend. I wondered if all this had been one huge lie.

"One more question, then," I said. "Why did Billy and the other guy—the Crutchfield fellow—why did they want to kill me? I'm assuming that's what they were trying to do?"

"I don't really know. It took me a while to come to my senses about Billy. I mean the gun and Moule and all was just so overwhelming that I almost couldn't comprehend that someone would put a gun in a human being's mouth and pull the trigger. I don't believe Billy's excuse about it being an accident. To answer your question, John, I think he was just mean. If his group couldn't have it, then no one else could either. The Bunker Hill guys have been known for their violence at times. So I cut him off. I wouldn't answer his calls. I guess he thought I'd cool down later, so he backed off and quit trying to get in touch with me." Sarah looked out toward the Atlantic. "He's dead now, though."

I followed her gaze eastward and saw a familiar figure in the distance looking in our direction, appearing to study the lighthouse through a pair of binoculars. Under the white Panama hat, behind the sunglasses, and despite the colorful Hawaiian shirt and knee-length Bermuda shorts camouflage, Labonsky was easily recognizable.

CHAPTER 35

Sarah apparently did not recognize Labonsky, or react in any way to suggest that she might have. She just continued to stare into the distance, evidently lost in thought. I said nothing. After a moment she turned to me and said, "Where do we go from here?" I didn't reply. She continued, "I'd like to see the money returned to its rightful owners. It looks like you're the only one that can make that happen."

"Yeah," I said. "And I want to be sure I get my finder's fee."

"I promised you that, didn't I?"

"You did, but we're talking about an account containing cryptocurrency, and we need to figure how to make the split."

For the first time since I'd met her, I read slight anger on Sarah's face. She briefly clenched her jaws, pursed her lips, and then said in a soothing voice that didn't at all match her body language, "I guess you're right. I'll run it by the group. We'll find a way."

"Okay, then. You'll be in touch?"

"In a day or two. We'll meet again, I guess for the last time." She rose and turned to go, but after a few steps turned back and sat down on the bench next to me. "But John, you hold the key to a lot of money. It might be possible for you and I, just the two of us, to put it to use, to accomplish some good in the world." She placed her hand on mine as she spoke.

"It's an idea," I said, my tone neutral. "Let's think about it and talk when we meet again."

Sarah smiled. "Good. I'll look forward to it." With that she rose and walked casually toward the parking lot.

I glanced at my watch. It was still not yet ten o'clock. My

meeting with Sarah had lasted less than an hour, but finally, and for the first time since Donald D'Entremont-Moule walked through the door of my gallery, I understood what was going on. Sarah McKinsey Scott—if that was in fact her real name—was a liar, a would-be thief, and a murderer. The preceding minutes I spent listening to her would have rated a Tony Award if presented on stage. Her performance, beautifully done, was a masterpiece of half-truths intertwined with self-serving lies. I imagined that what she said about Billy Jackson was probably correct, and that he was in fact the other man who died in the fiery wreck. He was also, no doubt, her partner in crime and likely the mastermind of a plot to steal Moule's millions. Sarah had referred several times to "the group." Sure, they might have actually been members of the alt-right activist groups, but I suspected much of that was merely window dressing for their cover story; I seriously doubted if any official had sanctioned their activities. Her closing ploy suggesting that she and I take off with Moule's money was utterly transparent in its insincerity. There was more that she didn't reveal, I was sure, but it was not pertinent to her current narrative. Those unknown factors were probably the basis of the FBI's interest and the reason she had not been arrested. She needed to be behind bars. Even though I was not officially involved in the investigation, I would now push to make that happen in the very near future.

It took me the better part of an hour to get back to the privacy of my apartment. I spent fifteen minutes or so calming down before I called Labonsky on his cell. "How'd it go?" he asked. "I kept a close eye on you two with my binoculars."

"Fine, I suppose. She's an articulate liar, but she answered some of my questions," I said.

"Some?"

"The ones she wanted to, I believe. I forgot to ask the name of the guy who planted the camera at my apartment, but I assume it was the same man who was with her at Moule's apartment."

"What did she say about that—about Moule's murder?" Labonsky asked.

"That it was an accident, more or less. That her friend—a guy named Billy Jackson—had stuck a pistol in Moule's mouth trying to make him talk after they drugged him with fentanyl and the gun sort of 'accidentally' fired. Sounded like unadulterated bullshit to me. Like 'Oh, yeah, we just came over to discuss things with him and in the process blew his head mostly off, but it was an accident, see, and we really didn't mean to do it because we're nice people and patriots at heart'—that kind of crap."

"Who is this Jackson fellow?" Labonsky sounded as if this name was new to him.

"Sarah's boyfriend, basically. But he's dead now."

"What the…?"

"Why don't we meet and talk? I want to see her behind bars, and I will do everything I can to make that happen. I can't arrest her; you can. Let me tell you the details in person. They'll be more than enough to arrest her on suspicion and hold her until you can get a judge to issue a formal warrant." We agreed to meet at my apartment after work.

Labonsky showed up about five-thirty this time, evidently believing that getting an update from me was more important than his dinner. "Tell me what happened," he said. "And don't spare the details. I hope I didn't make myself too obvious, but I had a clear view of you two just about every minute, first up on the lighthouse, and then later when you were sitting on the bench. If I'd been a lip reader I could have followed your conversation. Sarah didn't say anything, did she, like 'Someone's watching us,' or something?"

"Not at all. She seemed upset, and it appeared that she was trying to make me believe she was kind of a victim, that Moule's death was all her boyfriend's fault. But it was also strange that she didn't come across as being terribly upset about his death," I said.

"Boyfriend, eh?" Labonsky said, sounding surprised. "So we're dealing with more than one person then?"

"I don't know. Let me go over the conversation in detail and see what you think." I recounted the events of the morning, exactly quoting for Labonsky as much of the conversation as I could remember, ending with Sarah's suggestion that she and I grab the money and—I presumed—live happily ever after.

Labonsky listened quietly, then seemed pensive for a moment after I finished. "You know, you run across people like that, crazy people who could probably be successful in the world if they just did what the rest of us do, get a job, work for a living, get married maybe and raise a family. But no, some of them—and this Sarah girl sounds like one—have gotta live life on the edge. Lying, manipulating, cheating, stealing and worse. They get a thrill out of thinking they're smarter than the rest of us who stick to the straight and narrow. As my grandmother used to say, 'They'll lie when the truth will do.'" He shook his head.

"Seems that way," I said.

"Yeah, and a lot of them crash and burn"—Labonsky paused, then added—"in hell."

"What comes next?" I asked Labonsky. "I'm supposed to be giving Sarah the digital key to Moule's money—I guess that would be a flash drive or something similar. When she calls me back I'll be curious to hear what she's going to say about giving me my 'finder's fee.' And that's what worries me. If she didn't kill Moule herself, she's clearly an accomplice in his murder. I could imagine her doing the same to me for several million bucks. I think we're going to need lots of backup. How do you want to handle this?"

"I honestly don't know," Labonsky said. "You're right. It could be a real sticky situation. I'd like to think about it overnight, maybe toss some ideas back and forth with the other guys. My first thought is that you'd want to meet in a public place so our team could blend into the background. But then if there's any gunplay..." He didn't finish the sentence. "Or a more private place might work. We'd need a small but very select squad for that..." Again, he didn't finish the thought. "Let's talk about it tomorrow," he said, rising to leave. "You'll call me if you hear from Sarah?"

"I will," I said as Labonsky disappeared down my stairs and into the twilight. For some reason I felt sorry for him. He had nothing to go home to. But then, neither did I.

CHAPTER 36

I didn't sleep well; in fact it was something like 3:00 a.m. when I last recalled looking at the bedside clock. In the dark silence of my bedroom, an avalanche of thoughts and worries weighed down my ability to focus on any one of the multiple problems I needed to consider. What was Sarah's plan? I had to assume that she really believed I had acquired a way to access Moule's offshore millions, and that access was in the form of a digital key to an online account. In exchange for giving the key to her, I had asked for a cut, my "finder's fee." If that were the case, did she actually think I would be stupid enough to turn the key over to her and wait for a check to arrive in the mail? The most likely approach, from her perspective, was the one she suggested at the lighthouse, that we join forces, grab the money, and live happily ever after. Or something like that. Then she would disappear and leave me to face the consequences…

But none of that would happen. So far as I knew, there was no key or code or magic words that would open Moule's digital treasure chest. Sarah said that when she and Billy Jackson drugged him he said something like, "I gave the code to John O'Toole. He knows what I want." What did that mean? I had to presume he was talking about our arrangement to purchase investment-grade art, or something related to that. There was no other reasonable explanation. Moule had not—in any way, shape, or form—given me any code or key. I had no idea he planned to move his assets offshore. There was so much I didn't know, so many missing pieces of the puzzle.

All of this rumination was unnecessary. There would be no exchange. Sarah would call, and we would agree on a meeting site. We'd arrive, and shortly thereafter Labonsky and the

202

cops would swoop in and arrest her. From my perspective, the problem solved; the case closed; I get on with my life. With that assurance, I slept late the next morning and didn't make it to the gallery until nearly ten o'clock.

It was late afternoon before I heard from Labonsky. He said he had been trying to decide the best "and safest" location for Sarah and I to meet. "I don't expect any problems, but with situations like this, you've gotta be prepared. We'll all have guns, but I hope taking Ms. Sarah into custody doesn't require us to pull them out."

"So what have you come up with?" I asked.

"John, I think we want to do the arrest at your apartment," Labonsky said.

That idea had not occurred to me. Of all the places I might have considered, my apartment, my private space, would be at or near the bottom of the list. "Why there?" I asked.

"Think about it," Labonsky said. "We want a space whose entry and exit options are limited—in case someone tries to make a run for it. We want to be away from other people who might get hurt if there's gunfire. We want a place where we make the arrest with just a few experienced cops guarding the perimeter, something that won't alert the suspect or upset the neighborhood. Your place is ideal. There are two ways to get to the site, either from the gate to the alley or through the gallery—which will be closed at night, presuming that's when the collar takes place. Once in the courtyard, there is only one flight of steps up to your place—no back doors or the like, and I noticed when I was over there the other day that you have burglar bars on your windows. So one entry to the courtyard, one set of stairs, one front door. Simple and easy. Maybe four guys max to cover things."

"And how do you propose making the actual arrest?" I

asked. "Are you going to hide in the bedroom or a closet and jump out with a pistol in one hand and handcuffs in the other?"

"No, of course not. If Sarah's smart, she'll case the place as she arrives, and maybe even snoop around your apartment, checking to see if anyone's there. We'll hang back until she's inside with you, then close in and cover the courtyard and the gate."

"And then…?"

"I'll walk up the steps, knock on the door, you'll let me in and I'll arrest her."

"How do you know Sarah won't balk or try to run?"

"I don't, but I've been a cop for a long time. I know her type. She'll try to talk her way out of things before she'll run or do something crazy, like pulling a gun. It's gonna be an easy collar." Labonsky seemed to be waiting for my reply, but then added, "Oh, and when you talk with her, be sure she'll be coming by herself. If she wants to bring someone else with her, we'll need to rethink the whole plan."

"I'm thinking she'll want to come alone," I said, not mentioning my thoughts that she'd probably try to talk me into conspiring to take all of the money and split it with her. Once things got a tad difficult, it seemed Sarah had for the most part dropped the pretense that this money belonged to the Sojourners or the Bunker Hill crowd. What was it she'd said about "just the two of us" and accomplishing "some good in the world"? Good for who? Just the two of us, maybe? Now I had to wait for her call.

Two more days passed before the call came. "Hello, John," she said, sounding more familiar now. "I'm sorry I'm so slow getting back to you. I was trying to make some arrangements to get you paid." She seemed to hesitate and then said, "Listen, there have been some, er…complications, I guess you'd say. I

204

want to meet with you. I want to see you. I need to explain everything so you can help me decide what to do, what course we should take."

So it was "we" now, I thought. "Sure," I replied, deliberately sounding calm. "I'm in no rush. How about tomorrow night, say around nine?"

"Okay. Where shall we meet?" Sarah said. "Somewhere private, please."

"How about my apartment behind the gallery? I'll leave the back gate open."

"That's good. I'll call an Uber." She paused. "And John, let's take our time. I want to talk this thing through with you."

"Good. I'll see you tomorrow night about nine-ish," I said and hung up without giving her a chance to say more.

I immediately called Labonsky on his cell and told him the details of the planned meeting. "That gives us not much more than twenty-four hours. Short notice to set up a trap. I'll get right on it and start making some phone calls. And John, whatever you do, don't mention this to *anyone*," Labonsky said, emphasizing the last word. "In situations like this where there's big money involved, you can't be a hundred percent sure Sarah or one of her associates hasn't got a spy somewhere at headquarters who'll tip her off. It's happened before, believe me."

It was now a waiting game.

CHAPTER 37

The next day, a Thursday, dawned clear and somewhat cooler. I had been awake for more than an hour by the time the sun rose, nervously anticipating the events to come. If everything went as planned, by the next time I headed to bed, my life should be back on the road to normalcy. It turned out to be a routine day at the gallery. Labonsky called mid-afternoon to say that all was in place for our "meeting tonight at nine." Jessica asked for my help with a couple of large sales. As the business day drew to a close, she seemed quite happy. Hattie dropped by with the financial summary for the month just ended. Our sales were considerably better than a year earlier, with the outlook for the coming months a positive one. As we finished going over the report she remarked, "You seem a little distant, John; not your usual self. Anything we need to talk about?"

I smiled and said, "I'm sorry. Yeah, I've got a few things on my mind, but just personal stuff, nothing to do with the business."

"Well, you know I'm here if you need anything," Hattie said. Her voice was reassuring. Just give me twenty-four hours, I thought. Things will be fine.

I climbed the steps to my apartment just before six. I tried to read the news online but kept pacing about, wondering if I should be doing something—but I didn't know what. It crossed my mind that I should have a gun "just in case" the arrest went bad, but as a convicted felon I was not allowed to possess a firearm. I even briefly considered hiding a few steak knives in convenient spots around my living room, presumably where Labonsky would confront Sarah, but immediately dismissed the idea as silly and potentially dangerous. Seven became eight, and eight became eight-thirty. I unlocked the back gate facing the alley in anticipation of Sarah's arrival. The daylight was fading rapidly. By nine the only substantial illumination in the courtyard at the base of my staircase came from the lights on the rear of the gallery and the carriage house below my apartment. Pacing back and forth, I ventured out on the porch several times to see if I could spot any of Labonsky's men in the shadows. As far as I could tell, I was alone in the night. I sat on the sofa in my living room and waited, eyeing the clock on the opposite wall. At five past nine, I heard a soft knock on the door and turned to see Sarah standing outside.

I leaped up and opened the door. "I'm so sorry," I said. "I didn't hear you coming up the stairs."

Sarah smiled and said, "Someone once told me, 'When you're uncertain of where you're going, it's best to tread lightly.' It was good advice. I try to remember it." She was dressed this time in a white blouse and dark slacks, with a colorful scarf wrapped around her waist like a sash. She surveyed the room. "Do you mind if I look around?" she asked.

"Not at all," I said, smiling.

Moving quickly, Sarah peeked about and, apparently satisfied that we were alone, settled in my overstuffed armchair while waving me toward the sofa. "Let's talk," she said. The clock on the wall read 9:10. "For the past two days I've been trying to talk to the others about recovering the funds Moule took from us. They had initially agreed to your 'finder's fee,' as you called it, or a commission or small reward or whatever, but now they've changed their minds and want it all. And I hate that, John. You deserve something for all you've been through and—before you say I was the cause of a lot of it—I want to say I'm so very sorry. I didn't know you, I didn't understand who you are, but if I had, things would have been different. We've gotten off to a bad start. Before we go any further, I want to beg your forgiveness. Will you please forgive me?"

This had now become a game as far as I was concerned. Here was Sarah, reciting lines that I was sure she'd practiced and used before to gain the confidence of some reluctant man, yet perfectly willing to make a mockery of them when it suited her plans. It was a game two could play. "I don't know, Sarah," I said. "You, and your late friend Billy, have made my life miserable for these last months. You've made a fool of me and nearly got me killed. Why should I believe anything will be different in the future?" I quickly glanced at the clock. Where was Labonsky?

Sarah rose from the armchair and moved over to sit next to me on the sofa. Taking my hand and moving closer, she said, "Is there anything I can do to make it all up to you? Anything at all...?" Turning toward me now, she placed her other hand on my thigh just above my knee. The clock now read 9:16. Sarah was leaning closer when we heard a sound of footsteps on my porch. We both turned to look as Labonsky opened the door and strode in without knocking.

"Am I interrupting anything, boys and girls?" Labonsky asked, his voice sarcastic. "I've been standing outside there watching for the last few minutes. Reminded me of my high school years." Sarah backed away from me as I started to get up. "Keep your seat, John," he barked. Turning to Sarah he continued, "So I guess I've been dumped for someone else...?" he began.

"No! No! Rod, it's not that way," Sarah said. "John has the key. He knows how to get access to Moule's money. I was just trying to get him to see..."

Standing over us now, Labonsky reached out and slapped

her. "Shut up," he said. "I've had enough of your lies and bull-shit."

To that point, I had sat quietly in utter disbelief at what I was hearing. I looked at Labonsky. "Rod? You and Sarah...? How could you?"

"My wife left me...," he began.

"It wasn't that way," Sarah said, fear in her voice. Looking at me she continued, "After Moule's death we—Billy and me—were trying to understand how we could recover the money. There were two people who might know the answer—you, because of what Moule said, and Rod, because he was in charge of the investigation and had access to everything. Yes, I talked to both of you..."

"Talk's not the word, bitch," Labonsky said. "You fucked me and then made sure my wife found out so she'd leave me. You told me we would get our hands on the money and leave this town—see the world, you said. You had me believing for a while. I could make a new start. You tried to explain away the photo of you in bed with John, and I believed you because I wanted to. And then I heard about Billy...and I'm sure there are others, too." He reached behind him and drew a compact Glock automatic pistol from a holster on the rear of his belt.

"Where are your men, Rod? Where is your backup?" I asked, fearing the worst.

Labonsky smiled. "Just me tonight. Judge, jury, and executioner." He reached in his pants pocket and extracted a black cylindrical object that he quickly screwed on to the barrel of his pistol. "A silencer," he explained in response to my look. "So, John, let's start with you. I've believed all along that you're holding the key to Moule's money. You figured you could just lay low for a while till the cops lose interest in the case, then quietly get your hands on it. That was what our friend Sarah here suggested that *we*—she and I—do. Live the high life in Mexico or Europe or somewhere, but then…"

Labonsky's attention had been focused on me as he spoke. Sarah, seeing his distraction, leaped up and in two long steps was able to jerk open the door to the porch. The detective turned, calmly aimed, and fired twice just as she approached the top of the steps. The 9mm must have struck her directly in the spine about the level of her heart, as she pitched forward from the blow, fell onto the porch rail, and then somersaulted over to land in the courtyard below with a sickening thud. Turning back to me, Labonsky began, "Sorry about that, John. Now, where were we…?"

As the detective faced me, behind him a figure dressed in dark clothes appeared at the open door to the porch, weapon in hand. A familiar voice yelled, "Drop the gun and put your hands up, Labonsky."

Labonsky spun to face the intruder, still holding his pistol. Before he could lower his weapon, three quick shots struck him in the center of his chest, sending his body flying back to land next to me on the sofa as his weapon fell to the floor. With a gurgling sound, he appeared to take a deep breath, then stare upward before his head fell forward on his chest. Moving rapidly, Hasty kicked Labonsky's pistol out of reach as he holstered his weapon and asked almost calmly, "You okay, John?"

I looked to my left at Labonsky's lifeless body, blood still actively oozing from his chest wounds. The room was suddenly crowded with four additional men, each wearing a ballistic vest under a blue jacket with "FBI" emblazoned in large letters on the back. "I'm alive," I said.

"I'm sorry about how this has ended. It wasn't supposed to work out this way. We've been on to Labonsky and the Scott girl for a while now. There's a lot we've got to do, but I promise

I'll fill you in on all the details once the dust settles."

I sat there quietly on the sofa, not moving as the agents spoke on their phones to headquarters and to the Savannah police. For a moment, time seemed to stand still as the voices and hubbub in the background faded into an uninterpretable babble. Just give me twenty-four hours and everything will be fine, I had told myself. How could I have been such a fool?

EPILOGUE

It took a long time to recover from all that had happened. For months, visions of Labonsky's bloody corpse, Sarah's voice and the sound of her body hitting the flagstones in my courtyard, the artwork in Moule's house, and so on haunted my dreams almost nightly. Any sudden loud noise would bring forth images of Hasty firing his pistol. Many nights I would wake up in a cold sweat as my mind replayed one scene or another from what had been my life between the time I met Moule and the deaths of Rod Labonsky and Sarah Scott. I sought medical care, of course, and was referred to a psychiatrist who awarded me the diagnosis of PTSD—post-traumatic stress disorder. "We saw a lot of it after the Gulf War in the 1990s," he commented, as if my psychological kinship with battle-weary soldiers might bring some solace. I was prescribed antidepressants by day and sleeping meds at night with little symptomatic relief. I decided the treatment made me feel worse than the illness and stopped them all.

Finally, as the new year dawned, I began to feel some sense of regaining control and direction toward my version of normal. Jenna, who had been out of the picture for most of the "Moule months," as I took to calling them, stepped back into my life as my companion and psychological savior. She took a leave of absence from her job, asked her parents to care for her child, and was with me almost constantly for most of the first month. Hattie and Jessica saw to getting the mess and damage cleaned up and repaired in my apartment while Jenna and I stayed in a rented cabin down the coast on Sapelo Island. There, any news from Savannah was rarely if ever considered important.

Jim Hasty and Pete Marsh both came by to visit several times once the immediate issues relating to two law-enforcement shootings had died down. They both promised to answer my questions and fill me in on what I had missed, but wanted to wait until I was "less stressed," to use Marsh's term. Surprisingly, the Savannah news media had relatively little to say about either Sarah's or Labonsky's deaths. Both were said to be related to a "complex situation involving violations of both state and federal laws," and that Labonsky had served with the Savannah police for "several decades." There was no mention of the fact that Labonsky shot Sarah in cold blood and was then killed by FBI agents. I couldn't help but think that someone high up had asked the media to downplay the details of the story, even though the facts were readily available to a reporter willing to dig a bit.

Hasty's assignment in Savannah ended sometime in November, but he was frequently back and forth from his home in Atlanta for several months thereafter, "tying up loose ends," as he told me later. Shortly after Christmas he called and made an appointment to visit me in early January. On a clear but chilly afternoon, Hasty and Pete Marsh came by the gallery on Liberty Street, their first visit since completing the Labonsky investigation. We met in my private office.

"You're looking good," Hasty said, trying to break the ice in what was otherwise an awkward situation. It was hard to see him in person again without remembering the night he shot and killed Labonsky. "John, I'm sorry you got caught up in all of this. You're as much of a victim as anyone."

"Maybe," I said, trying to sound upbeat, "but things are getting better. Business is good, and I'm almost back to my old self. Time does wonders."

"Let me generally go over the investigation and then

answer any questions you have. I promised that I would, so here we are," Hasty said. Pete Marsh was silent but nodded agreement. "First, about Sarah Scott. She was a small-town girl who moved to the big city and never looked back. Her family is from Valdosta in south Georgia, and as I think you know, she was into video gaming big time. You said she gave you some song and dance about being in college in California and having a master's degree from Georgia State and being divorced and all that." I nodded. "Like most other things in the poor girl's life, it was a pack of lies. She did a couple of years of college in her hometown, then moved to Atlanta and was in and out of trouble. I think she told you she'd gotten a divorce and moved to Savannah? Actually, she'd never been married—not that we know of, anyway—and was in federal prison in Marianna, Florida, just before she came to Savannah. She'd been convicted as an accessory to a bank robbery that earned her three years of hard time. While she was in prison—and maybe before—she got involved with some radical groups, white supremacist types who both advocated and committed violence against anyone they considered 'foreign.' Neo-Nazi types. And she took up with another member, Billy Jackson, who also had a long rap sheet. One joined the Bunker Hill gang and the other the Sojourners, but both were looking to recruit members to form their own group. To do that they needed money. This thing with Moule came up and they figured if they could get their hands on it they'd be fixed. All this stuff she told you about consulting with 'others' was just crap. For most of the time it was just her and Billy Jackson."

"Did you know at first that he'd been killed in the wreck?" I asked.

"No. We ID'ed the driver, the Crutchfield guy, pretty quickly. It took us a while to realize the other fellow was

Jackson. There wasn't much left of him after the fire."

"But why were they trying to kill me?"

"As best I understand it, they weren't. They were planning to kidnap you and force you to give them the key to Moule's money. After the accident, Sarah didn't spend too much time mourning—she decided she'd get the key herself by using her 'feminine wiles,' to use the old term. She was with Billy when they drugged you. Then she went after Labonsky. He and his wife were going through a rough patch. He got in the habit of drinking in a certain bar most nights..."

"The Sandfly Lounge off Abercorn?" I asked.

"Yeah, how'd you know?"

"Long story—but go on with what you were saying."

"Well, anyway Sarah found out he was the lead detective on the Moule case, so she just happens to be there in the bar and meets him. They drink a bit, and she suggests going somewhere 'private.' Labonsky's wife was staying at her mother's for the weekend so, fool that he was, he takes Scott to his house and has sex with her in his own bed, and then she 'accidentally' leaves a set of lacy panties between the sheets, and when the wife comes back home...well, you can figure what happened, and by then Sarah owns Labonsky, who's about old enough to be her father." Hasty stopped and took a deep breath. "And you know it was his wife that ratted him out to us?"

"No," I said, surprised. I hadn't heard that part of the story.

"So we knew they—Rod and Ida, that's the wife's name— were separated, but we didn't know why. He didn't volunteer any info, and nobody around the station thought it was their place to ask. Ida moved in with her mother but still had most of her clothes and things at their house—where Rod was living. About five or six weeks before the"—he hesitated—"the end, she went over to their house to get some of her things. It was about nine o'clock in the evening if I remember correctly. Rod was drinking kind of heavy then—most nights in the bar—and he'd come home and crash in bed early to sober up for the next day. Well, she sees his truck in the driveway, and since she had a key to the house, she lets herself in the carport door. She could hear Rod snoring on the couch in the family room in the back of the house, and sort of sticks her head in to tell him she's there, but he's out cold from the booze. About that time she hears a phone buzzing and looks on the coffee table and sees two cell phones, one she recognized as the one issued through work and the other she doesn't recognize. And that's the one that's buzzing. Rod's out cold so she picks it up and sees he has a text message. She clicks on the icon and finds a whole long series of sexy texts from someone named Sarah. She told us she read some of them but got so sick and upset that she couldn't finish them all. But the important thing was that several of the texts were about the Moule investigation.

"Ida didn't know what to do. She loved her husband and was hoping they could get back together, but the details in the texts were just too much. She brooded and worried for a couple of weeks, then finally went to her priest and told him the whole story. He had her do a bunch of 'Hail Marys' and told her she was morally obligated to report it to the police if Rod was sharing confidential information with someone not in law enforcement. So she called Pete Marsh, and then I got involved. Rod was still using his department-issued phone, so we didn't need a warrant to track him and eavesdrop on his conversations. One of them turned out to be a call between you two about arresting Sarah at your apartment. The thing was, though, no one in the department—especially those of us on the Moule case—knew anything about it. That's why I took over and

216

brought the team in from the FBI," Hasty said.

"Yeah, I understand that now," I said. "I realized Labonsky was on his own when he said he was the 'judge, jury, and executioner.'"

I ended up talking with Hasty and Marsh for another hour. Most of my questions were answered, at least as much as I wanted to know. Both men thanked me for the assistance I'd tried to give them before things blew up.

As the two rose to leave, Pete Marsh, who had said little during the entire visit, spoke. "Uh…to sort of show our appreciation for all your help, and by way of apology for all you've been through, we brought you a small gift. It's out in the car, if you'll give me a minute to bring it in."

Marsh stepped out to the courtyard and returned a few minutes later carrying a large flat object covered with black plastic sheeting. He carefully set one end on the floor. "I guess you realize we've cleared the Moule murder case. Both Billy Jackson and Sarah Scott are dead. She more or less confessed to you, and all the evidence supports her account of what happened. The DA feels there's nothing more to prosecute so he closed the file. Well, if you remember, there was this painting that Moule had in his bedroom. It was wrapped up in brown paper and had a note saying he was giving it to you. I guess he intended to do that when you came over for your appointment that Saturday afternoon and found him dead. We aren't too sure who owns Moule's house or the rest of his estate since he died without a will, but this was clearly yours, and the Chief and the DA have signed off on us giving it to you." With that, he pulled back the tape holding the plastic cover to reveal Moule's Rothko painting.

I was stunned, so much so that I found myself at a loss for words. "That's…that's…wonderful," I stammered. "Thank you. Thank you so much." I reached out and touched the edge of the painting, almost trying to assure myself that it was real. "Are you sure about this…?" I started to ask.

"Yes," Marsh said, handing me a thick envelope. "We had one of the Superior Court judges formally sign off on the transfer of the title to the painting. It's all in there, signed, sealed, and duly recorded in the Chatham County courthouse."

For the next hour after Hasty and Marsh left, I sat in my office and stared at the painting. Did they have any idea how much the painting was worth? Did they care? But why had Moule wanted to give it to me in the first place? I assumed I would never know. I stood up, straightened my shirt, went in my private bathroom, splashed water on my face and ran a comb through my hair. I then opened my office door and called for Jessica. I decided at that very moment that I had put it all behind me, that I had obtained what is vaguely referred to as "closure." I was back to myself.

For the next week, the Rothko sat propped up against the wall in my private office, still wrapped in its black plastic cover. One by one I showed it to Jessica, to Hattie, to Phil Holloway, and to Jenna, each of them marveling at my new possession. In truth, I wasn't sure what to do with it. Assuming the validation by the National Gallery in Washington was legit, the piece would sell for more than a million dollars at auction. I began to worry about an accidental fire or burglars or vandals and all the other things that might or possibly could happen to this incredibly valuable bit of canvas dabbed with paint. Again, I thought of Moule, not in a bad way this time, but of what he said about works of art not being "real," of how we agree to assign values to physical or digital objects based on our agreed perceptions, not on some objective utilitarian worth. Things like cryptocurrency. Or paintings by Mark Rothko.

More than a month passed as the plastic-covered million-dollar painting remained propped against the wall. I couldn't decide what to do with it. Should I sell it, or give it to a museum, or store it in a disaster-proof vault somewhere? I believe it was the painting's association with Moule that made me hesitate. Even though I was feeling pretty much back to normal now, I didn't know exactly how to deal with this graphic reminder of the recent past events. Jessica solved the problem for me, barging into my office one Monday morning to demand in no uncertain terms that I either get rid of the Rothko or hang it on the wall for everyone to see. "I'm getting tired of seeing that lump of black plastic taking up space in your office."

She was right. I needed to move on, to bury my equivocation. "Okay," I said, almost without thinking. "Let's hang it here behind my desk for everyone to see."

"Great," Jessica said. "We'll do that at lunchtime. Why don't you get it out of that plastic wrap and see if it's got a hanging wire on the back?" She headed back to the front desk, smiling at having prodded me to action.

I rolled my desk chair over by the painting and sat in it while I carefully removed its plastic cover. It was a beautiful piece, no doubt, Rothko's marvelous mélange of color, shape, and texture that set the standard for generations of artists to follow. As with all of his major paintings, the work was unframed. The canvas lapped over the edges of the wooden stretcher frame a full two inches and was painted in the same hue as the adjacent face of the work. On the back, a rugged wire was attached to sturdy D-ring hangers, each affixed with two screws into the frame. No problem, I thought. Then I saw it.

Just at the level where the hanging wire was attached, a

small flat object appeared to be wedged between the face of the canvas and the frame. Only a millimeter or two was visible; at first I thought this was a piece of trash that had somehow gotten lodged there over the years. I pulled out my cell phone and pressed the flashlight icon to get a better look. The object was less than half an inch wide, and appeared new against the half-century-plus age of the painting. Carefully, I teased it out with my fingernail. It was a microSD card. I felt my heart pounding and started to call Jessica, but immediately thought better of it.

Rolling my chair back behind my desk, I inserted the card in the appropriate slot in the side of my laptop computer. A directory window popped up. I clicked on the listing for the card. It appeared to contain a single file, a PDF named simply "Letter to JO." I double-clicked the file name and the document appeared on my screen. It was a brief letter about a planned conversation that never took place:

> John,
> As we discussed, I have been forced to make some major unanticipated changes in my dealings with clients. Yesterday, I moved my accounts to a unit of Swissbanc in the Cayman Islands. I need more security and less government scrutiny. With that said, I want to proceed ahead with our planned purchases of quality art. I know funds will be required, often on short notice, so I have opened a joint account in both of our names at the bank, funding it initially with $2.5 million. You should have no problem accessing this. I will leave it to your discretion to proceed with the first purchases. The information on the attached page lists the account number and the necessary verification codes to make withdrawals or transfers from this account. I have also given you the name and private phone number of my banker there should you have any questions or difficulties.

I apologize for this inconvenience, and want to thank you for all of your assistance.

Don Moule

I couldn't believe what I was reading. Moule was murdered on the day he was scheduled to meet with me. He had set up a joint account in my name with $2,500,000 and given me apparent free rein to spend it on art as we had discussed. He trusted me. I stared at the screen, reading and rereading Moule's letter.

After what seemed like an eternity, I closed the file, pulled the memory card out of my laptop, and opened the door to my private bathroom. There I tossed the card in the toilet and flushed it, watching to be sure it disappeared into Savannah's sewer system. I then opened my office door and called out to Jessica, telling her I was ready to hang the painting. And about the future, not the past.

Moule's Rothko still hangs behind my desk. I see it there almost every day and wonder occasionally if in fact it is the work of the artist or just a copy by a talented forger. I have the authentication documents from the National Gallery, but they, too, could be forgeries. There is no doubt I could resolve the question with a simple phone call or email, but given the choice between knowledge and belief, I have chosen to suppose that this work of art is—to use Moule's term—"real."

ACKNOWLEDGMENTS

Many things factor into the writing of a work of fiction, not the least of which are the persons and situations that inspire and assist the creative process. In appreciation, I want to express my gratitude to the good people at Mercer University Press for their support of my writing and their input and assistance when needed. I am also thankful for the persons, places, and situations that over the years have stimulated my imagination, leading to tales such as this one. Especial thanks are due to Allen Hodges for his review of the manuscript and valuable input thereon.